I0771709

Mrs. Nash

A Screenplay by

Ruth J. Heflin

Mrs. Nash was first published in *Rushing Thru the Dark,* Autumn 2024.

Printed and bound in the United States of America.
A product of Kansas.

ISBN 979-8-9911790-7-2

Other Works by Ruth J. Heflin

*Pitiless Bronze: A Postpatriarchal
Examination of Prepatriarchal Cultures*

*I Remain Alive: the Sioux
Literary Renaissance*

*Freddi Flies:
A Children's First Time Flying Adventure*

*Time Coven: Tales f Space, Magic,
and Time Travel*

*Facts Patriarchists
Don't Want You to Know*

Yonni Hale and the Cosmic Wind
(pseudonym Rajah Hill)

A dramatization of
the first historically documented
EuroAmerican male
to live his life as a woman
in the United States of America
in the style of Alfred Hitchcock

Dedicated to Leonard Leff,
Author of *Hitchcock and Selznick*,
and one of the best professors
I ever knew
who knew when to use expletives
and when not to

MRS. NASH ii

Foreword

The phenomenon of biological males defining themselves as female is nothing new. Historical records prove that at least a few males transformed into females at least 5000 years ago.

For millennia, humans have been told males are "superior" to females in almost every way, but most women have long known this myth to be the lie that it is. This myth, what I call the Male Myth, is an artifice that props up patriarchies, but the only way they can make that myth seem like reality is to deny women educations, to deny women access to healthy exercise and competitive sports, and to deny women work experiences that enhance their natural talents and intelligence. Without these limitations, women thrive everywhere.

Beneath the Male Myth is another secret that patriarchists do not want us to know—that Feminine Power is real.

In fact, before 2400 BCE when the Egyptians discovered that males actually do play a physical role in pregnancy, as I discuss in my book *Pitiless Bronze: A Postpatriarchal Examination of Prepatriarchal Cultures*, women created and ran everything—their own households, their own industries, cities and even nations.

Undeniably, women were The Creators—from bringing new life into this world through a monthly battle with the cosmos (from whence comes menstrual blood) to designing and building the houses every family lived in, hence the title "homemaker."

Given irrefutable facts, such as the fact that pound-for-pound women are physically stronger than men, ancient men were so intimidated by the power women, especially the women who ran the cities' temples, wielded that they steadily began doing everything they could, after learning they play a role in pregnancy, to make themselves "transcendent" above women, including demoting goddesses and taking over the running of those temples. Akhenaten, the Egyptian pharaoh, even had himself depicted as femininely as possible in order to compete with the God's Wife, the woman in charge of the Temple of Aten, arguably more wealthy and powerful than the king himself.

If the Male Myth is still so widely believed, why, then, do so many biological males desire to be or feel as though they are women? What is this Power of the Feminine they are so attracted to?

The story of Mrs. Nash was told in two sources of the time period, including in a book by Lizzie Custer, George Custer's wife (herein called Libby). One newspaper article in the *Bismarck Tribute*, November 4, 1878, though conflates her life with that of Mrs. Noonan, another trans woman at Fort Lincoln (?), reportedly citing marriage certificates as proof. As such, both Mrs. Nash and Mrs. Noonan are the oldest verifiable account of any EuroAmerican men who lived their lives as women.

It's time to reclaim the Power of the Feminine by acknowledging trans people's rights as human beings.

Ruth J. Heflin, November 6, 2024

Abbreviations in Screenplays

CONT = continue (meaning the person
speaking continues to speak)
EXT = exterior shot
INT = interior shot

FADE IN:

INT FORT RILEY OFFICERS BALLROOM
EVENING
The year is 1878. A military band plays, and a
young tenor sings, "I'll Take You Home Again,
Kathleen" by Thomas P. Westendorf, as Cavalry
officers mingle and dance with colorfully
dressed women. MARIA STRAW and CAPT.
BENJAMIN STRAW are in attendance. Flags
and displays of arms festoon the room, which
isn't crowded since only a sprinkling of people
have shown up. One woman in her mid-thirties,
MRS. NASH, because she is tall, angular, yet
attractive, stands out. She finishes a dance with
a young officer, and, at her request, they move
over to the refreshment table. She motions
toward a chair, moving to sit in it rather quickly.
People notice. She smiles and waves off
attention, gratefully accepting the punch her
young officer hands her. She sips the punch,
pulls out her fan and tries to appear well, but her

hands tremble. Making excuses, MRS. NASH leaves the room.

EXT VERANDA OUTSIDE BALLROOM EVENING
MRS. NASH makes her way slowly down the veranda outside the ballroom, past one or two people, to the stairs. She stops, steadies herself, and leans heavily on the rail as she descends the stairs.

INT THE BALLROOM EVENING
The dancing continues.

EXT FORT RILEY PARADE GROUNDS EVENING
MRS. NASH crosses the grounds, still alone, slowly.

INT THE BALLROOM EVENING
The dancing continues.

EXT WASHINGTON AVENUE, FORT RILEY EVENING
We see the street and yard in front of a large stone townhouse. Gas lamps are lit along the street. MRS. NASH makes her way across the yard and up the steps, pausing only briefly on the stairs—obviously in physical discomfort.

INT THE BALLROOM SAME EVENING
The dancing continues. A younger, heavy-set woman, MARIA STRAW, moves over and whispers to her husband, CAPT. BENJAMIN STRAW, who is standing with other officers. He distractedly waves her on her way. She hurriedly yet taking the time to smile politely at people she

passes, leaves through the same door MRS. NASH did.

INT BEDROOM SAME EVENING
MRS. NASH pours water from a pitcher and tries to cool her head and wrists. Sitting on the edge of the bed, she bends over to pull off her button-up shoes. Dizzy, she straightens up trying to regain her balance, instead falls forward onto the floor.

EXT PORCH ROOF OF TOWNHOUSE
SAME EVENING
We see through the second story window, having a view of the top half of the staircase, all of the hallway, and part of the bedroom interior. MARIA mounts the stairs and turns down the hallway. She enters the bedroom, finds MRS. NASH prostrate, while we see only part of MRS. NASH's body; the rest is obscured by the view of the bed. MARIA bends down to check her. The singing and music, which have been heard all this time, stop.

                    MARIA
                  (groaning)
        Oh, no.

INT FORT RILEY UNDERTAKER'S
WORKROOM MORNING
The room is brightly lit by windows on two sides. The floors are wooden and heavily worn. The walls are white washed, but there is no air of sterility or particular cleanliness to the room. The military UNDERTAKER, a young staff sergeant who looks very boyish, almost effeminate, is finishing his breakfast and humming the hymn, "Hiding in Thee" by Ira

David Sankey and William O. Cushing, as he enters the room.

The UNDERTAKER sets the remainder of his egg sandwich on the sheet covering the corpse of MRS. NASH, which is on the table in the center of the room, as he pulls the sheet partly down to reveal the face. His hand scrapes against what feels like stubble. He looks closer at the corpse's face and is briefly puzzled by what appears to be beard growth.

He checks the slip of paper under MRS. NASH's head, then seems to almost smile as he runs a finger down the jaw line. Holding the egg sandwich in his mouth, he pulls the sheet the rest of the way off. As he finishes the sandwich, he removes her shoes, already partly undone, then moves to the top of the table to begin unbuttoning her dress. He notices a similar stubble on the chest, and a notable absence of breasts, just stuffing inside the corset. Presently, he removes the underwear and his suspicions are confirmed.

                    UNDERTAKER
                (with a quiet laugh)
          So, Mrs. Nash, you are a man.

INT A DARKENED BEDROOM IN BOSTON, MASS.--1873 NIGHT
A placard should indicate that it is Five Years Earlier.

The sounds of lovers accompany the movement of sheets, slightly obscured by the large bedposts and drapes of a canopy bed. The bedroom door opens suddenly and light stabs across the bed.

ABRAHAM WRIGHT (OS)
Claypool? Clay, is that you?
A man, ABRAHAM WRIGHT, in his 50s enters the room with a candelabra in one hand and a pistol in the other. He approaches the bed, where the sounds and movements have stopped.

ABRAHAM (CONT)
I know you're there, Claypool Wright.
Show yourself like a man.

A young, lightly bearded man in his early 20s, CLAYPOOL WRIGHT, gets out of the bed and stands beside the backside of the bed, covering himself with a sheet. The bed's other occupant remains completely covered.

ABRAHAM (CONT)
I knew it, you...you...bastard.

No, I can't call you that; it'd dishonor
the woman who bore you.

ABRAHAM begins to circle the bed, trying to direct the light from the candelabra to get a view of the young man and the bed's other occupant, who remains hidden in the dark under the covers. CLAYPOOL/CLAY approaches him, holding out a hand as if to stop him.

CLAYPOOL WRIGHT
Father, don't. You don't understand.

ABRAHAM

Don't call me that. You're no son of
mine.

                    CLAY
Don't....It's not like you think. It's...

                  ABRAHAM
You...you...sodomite. You'll pay for your
sins. Both of you will pay.

ABRAHAM turns the pistol toward the figure
sitting under the sheets and fires. The figure
under the sheet drops to the bed. CLAY lunges
for the gun, struggling to wrestle it out of his
father's hand. The candelabra drops to the floor.
ABRAHAM screams as though burned,
releasing the gun in his effort to get away from
his son's touch. He continually wipes his hands
over his arms and hands where CLAY touched
him.

               ABRAHAM (CONT)
Don't ever come near me again. Don't
ever look at me again. As far as I'm
concerned, you're dead.

ABRAHAM runs from the room. CLAY turns
toward the bed, picking up the candelabra to see
better. A man in his 40s, PROFESSOR
EDWARD NEISMAN, shivers there, unharmed
by the bullet. He reaches for CLAY. They
embrace.

EXT HARVARD GROUNDS DAY
Snow covers the ground. Sidewalks are shoveled
clean. CLAY, a long dark coat wrapped about
him, waits on a bench. NEISMAN, wearing a
black don's robe and carrying a large black

valise, exits a building and heads in CLAY's direction. They walk across the grounds together. Their breath steams as they talk.

CLAY
(gravely)
Leaving?

NEISMAN
Voluntarily removing myself from the esteemed, and enlightened, Harvard grounds.
(looks around)
Not that I want to teach here now. I won't teach anywhere in New England again.

CLAY
What will you do? You can't go south.

NEISMAN
No, I'll probably head west. California maybe. And you?

CLAY
Father's cut off my income, but Mother sent me enough to last a while. I can't...go anywhere else.

NEISMAN
How will you support yourself?

CLAY
My best friend, Charles Stallard, has agreed to let me stay with him for a while. His parents have always been fond of me. I can probably manage for some time.

                    NEISMAN
          And if they find out?

                    CLAY
          Try to convince them it's not true.

                    NEISMAN
                    (stops)
          Can you convince yourself? You know
          you can't live without...X, as
          Tchaikovsky calls it. You haven't chosen
          it; it's chosen you. You'll want such a
          relationship, as we had, again. You know
          you will.

                    CLAY
                    (uncomfortable)
          I'm not like you. I don't need...anything.
          I'll get along just fine.

NEISMAN looks at him skeptically and steps
into a waiting carriage. CLAY watches the
carriage leave before crossing the street.

EXT BOSTON OPERA HOUSE NIGHT
Snow falls. Carriages pull up and release
extravagantly dressed occupants. CLAY, with a
young woman on his arm (TILLY OSGOOD),
disembarks behind another couple (CHARLES
STALLARD and DATE). They enter.

INT ENTRANCE HALL OF OPERA HOUSE
CLAY checks his hat and coat at the cloak room,
flirting with the COAT CHECK GIRL. Takes
TILLY's arm again. An older man, recognizing
CLAY, stops, watches CLAY, whispers to his
wife, and hustles her inside while she tries to
look at CLAY. CHARLES notices the attention.

                    CHARLES
                 (nudging Clay)
Did you see that? Old Professor Hill
seemed to sniff something peculiar.

        (CHARLES indicating TILLY)
You haven't tainted this young woman's
reputation already, have you?

                     CLAY
                  (smiles)
No, not yet.

                    TILLY
                 (giggles)
Oh, stop it, you two. Professor Hill was
probably just noticing my new fur. He's
probably the old stuffy type who doesn't
think young women should dress so
flashily.

                   CHARLES
        (smiling and winking at CLAY)
Yes, I'm sure you're right. How could
anyone think Mr. Claypool Wright had
anything but honorable intentions
toward any woman?

EXT OUTSIDE A BOSTON BALLROOM
NIGHT
Carriages pull up and release extravagantly
dressed occupants.

INT ENTRYWAY TO A BOSTON BALLROOM
NIGHT
CLAY, TILLY, CHARLES and a NEW DATE
enter boisterously, shaking snow off their coats.
All check their apparel with an ATTENDANT
and enter the main ballroom.

INT MAIN BALLROOM SAME NIGHT
CLAY and TILLY begin to dance immediately to
a Tchaikovsky waltz. CHARLES and his DATE
separate--she heads toward a group of women,
he to a group of men.

CHARLES' DATE enters the group of six
women, all in their late teens, early twenties,
exuberantly.

                FIRST WOMAN IN GROUP
          Don't tell us you came here with them.

                CHARLES' DATE
          With whom?

                SECOND WOMAN
          With Claypool Wright and his lot.

                CHARLES' DATE
                    (puzzled)
          Yes, of course.

                FIRST WOMAN
          Poor thing. Haven't you heard?

CHARLES nonchalantly lights a cigar before
approaching his cronies, six men about his own
age.

FIRST MAN
How is everything, Stallard?

CHARLES
Fine, Wallace. And you?

SECOND MAN
Still faithful to Wright, I see.

CHARLES
Faithful?

FIRST MAN
Oh, come now, Stallard. Surely, you've
heard the rumors.

CHARLES
Since when do you listen to gossip,
Wallace?

THIRD MAN
Claypool Wright is a fine young man,
I'm sure. But you know how rumors
thrive in Boston. Wagging tails keep
tales wagging, if you know what I mean.

CLAY and TILLY finish a waltz and move toward
the refreshment room. People watch them,
moving out of their way politely.

INT REFRESHMENT ROOM   SAME NIGHT

TILLY
(giggles)
They think we're a scandal, don't they?

CLAY
Does that bother you?

                    TILLY
No, except that...

                    CLAY
Except that, what?

                    TILLY
Father says I shouldn't see you anymore.
He says he doesn't like the way people
are beginning to talk about you.

                    CLAY
           (feigning innocence)
About me?

                    TILLY
I suppose you've tarnished too many
women's reputations.

                    CLAY
You don't seem to mind.

                    TILLY
I've never been noticed this much
before. I always feel as though I'm
somebody with you.

                    CLAY
           (looking around)
As you are, Tilly.

       (CLAY in a fierce whisper)
And what would you do if I kissed you
right now?

                    TILLY
I'd...blush. But I'd probably love it.

CLAY sweeps TILLY into an elaborate embrace and kiss. Many people watch, some with elaborate disgust, others with obvious relief and amusement. CHARLES watches from just inside the doorway.

INT DINING ROOM OF STALLARD MANSION EVENING
Large, dark, heavy drapes completely cover large windows along one side of the room. A fairly long table, ornately set and surrounded by high-backed Victorian furniture, and a long sideboard along the wall opposite the windows, completely covered by silver trays laden with food, take up a good deal of the room. A large marble fireplace fills the end opposite the double doorway. A BUTLER slides the doors open, and several well-dressed people enter and find their specified seats around the table. CLAY has TILLY and another YOUNG WOMAN on each arm. CHARLES is escorting his MOTHER and another OLDER WOMAN. MR. STALLARD is talking with his COLLEAGUE, the older woman's husband.

                    MR. STALLARD
          Louisiana's sugar crop this year was less
          than a third what it was twenty years
          ago. Charles says what with all the
          negroes moving north and west to find
          employment there's no one to work the
          fields anymore.

                    COLLEAGUE
          If Hawaii hadn't increased its
          production, prices would be soaring
          now.

MRS. STALLARD
Yes, but do we want to eat sugar made at
a place filled with so many lepers?

CHARLES
Now, mother. I've told you the lepers are
separate from the cane growers.

CLAY
What we really have to worry about are
these Populists.

MR. STALLARD
Poor Southerners who've moved West
for free land. Free land. You'd think the
government had more sense. Some of
them have got so much land now they
think they're rich men.

TILLY
I thought having land meant they were
rich.

Everyone pauses to look at TILLY. The older
men smile at her politely. CHARLES looks at her
as though she's meddled again, then looks at
CLAY, who smiles and shrugs. MRS.
STALLARD looks around the table, wiping her
mouth with her napkin, then motions for the
BUTLER to bring more food from the sideboard.

COLLEAGUE
(under his breath)
Having land didn't help the Indians.

INT DRAWING ROOM OF THE STALLARD
MANSION NIGHT
The men, CHARLES, his father, CLAY, and
another man, have been smoking after dinner.
CHARLES' father engages the fourth man in
moderate conversation as they are seated in
comfortable chairs near the fireplace.
CHARLES and CLAY have been standing,
leaning against the backs of tall chairs, at a
respectable distance, listening to the two older
men converse. CLAY exhales cigar smoke and
nods toward the two older men.

                    CLAY
          That's how we'll be some day.

                    CHARLES
               (as out of a reverie)
          Excuse me?

                    CLAY
          Like them. Two old men contemplating
          the demise of the world over good cigars
          as our dinners digest.

                    CHARLES
          Yes, possibly.

               (looks CLAY over seriously)
          You think we'll be...friends, I mean, as
          good of friends as we are now...always?

                    CLAY
               (shifting closer, affectionately)
          Don't you?

                    CHARLES
          (motioning CLAY further from the fire)

Not that I mind, you understand, but
father's been worrying at me about it. I
mean it doesn't look good for him to
take in a young man of question-able
reputation, you know. Especially with
your father being a respectable lawyer, a
partner of Leeds, Carey, and Wright,
after all. Mr. Wright's judgment isn't
likely to be questioned, and father's
concerned how he, how he and I...

                    CLAY
                  (curtly)
What is it, Charles?

                  CHARLES
Is there any chance of your father's
taking you back?

                    CLAY
                (stiffening)
No. None. I've told you that before.
Look, as soon as I get taken on by a firm,
I'll leave. I know I've been a financial
burden to you and your father, but...

                  CHARLES
It's not that.

                    CLAY
What then?

                  CHARLES
Don't you know?

                    CLAY
Don't I know what?

                    CHARLES
          People have been talking.

                     CLAY
          Yes, well, I know people are unkind
          about my financial situation, but...

                    CHARLES
          No, it's more than that.

                     CLAY
          What then?

                    CHARLES
          There's talk that you were expelled from
          Harvard for...well, for
          some...unsavory...actions.

                     CLAY
          Unsavory?

CHARLES steps closer. Their voices take on a
more intimate tone as they occasionally glance
toward the older men.

                    CHARLES
          Were you involved with Professor
          Neisman?

                     CLAY
          Involved?
                    CHARLES
              (almost conspiratorially)
          Were you?

CLAY smiles and takes a long drag from his
cigar.

MONTAGE:
EXT OUTSIDE BOSTON OPERA HOUSE
NIGHT
CHARLES and a new date disembark a cab.
Snow on the ground shows signs of beginning to
melt away.

INT JUST INSIDE OPERA ENTRANCE
SAME NIGHT
CLAY is checking his hat and coat, as TILLY
stands by. TILLY smiles happily at CHARLES,
as he and his date enter, and waves. CHARLES
maneuvers his date over to the other side of the
entrance. CLAY escorts a puzzled TILLY inside.
INT MAIN BALLROOM NIGHT
CLAY and TILLY enter. Everyone seems to stop
and   stare.   TILLY   beams;   CLAY   is
uncomfortable. They head to the refreshment
room and people part noticeably to get out of
their way.

EXT OUTSIDE THE OSGOOD
BROWNSTONE NIGHT
CLAY rings the bell. A MAID answers. Shakes
her head. He becomes insistent. She starts to
close the door on him. He tries to stop her. A
BUTLER   intervenes,   imposingly.   CLAY,
disgusted, leaves. TILLY watches from an upper
window.

EXT OUTSIDE THE BOSTON OPERA
HOUSE NIGHT
It's raining heavily, but the flow of patrons is as
heavy as ever. CLAY disembarks a cab, but he is
stopped by a DOOR ATTENDANT. After a brief
discussion, the ATTENDANT steps away to help
someone else exit a cab. Dumbfounded because
he's been told not to enter, CLAY stands out in

the rain. Eventually moving away because people begin to stare.

EXT OUTSIDE THE BOSTON BALLROOM
NIGHT
The pre-spring wind is heavy, causing skirts to flap like flags. CLAY disembarks a cab and is greeted by coldness from other patrons, none of whom return his greetings.

INT ENTRYWAY TO BALLROOM SAME
NIGHT
Even the COAT CHECK GIRL is cool toward him. People make an obvious effort not to be near him.

INT MAIN BALLROOM SAME NIGHT
CLAY approaches a group of young men, who make an obvious effort to shun him. Across the room, TILLY, who is with CHARLES, muffles tears in a handkerchief as she's escorted into another room. She looks longingly after CLAY. An ATTENDANT approaches CLAY with his coat. The ATTENDANT starts an explanation, but CLAY waves him off in disgust. With one last look around, CLAY takes his coat, tosses it over one arm, and steps out into the wind.

EXT THE RED LIGHT DISTRICT OF
BOSTON NIGHT
CLAY, slightly tipsy, walks down the street looking closely at all the women. One woman, VERA, nearly as tall as CLAY and large boned (she should have strongly "masculine" features), attracts his attention the most. CLAY follows her actions from across the street, not certain she's a prostitute. She smiles at a man passing by. He ignores her. She fluffs up her the flounced

material on her dress' bustle, and notices CLAY watching her. Placing her hands firmly on her hips, she begins to swing them as she walks down the street. Finally, he approaches her.

                    CLAY
          Excuse me, madam. Are you a lady of
          the evening?

                    PROSTITUTE
               (doesn't lose a beat)
          It's evening, isn't it? And I'm obviously a
          lady. Right?

                    CLAY
               (looks her over)
          Well...

                    PROSTITUTE
            (straightening to her full height)
          What do you mean, well?

                    CLAY
               (backs up a bit)
          Of course, madam. I only meant to say
          that...that...you're a very striking
          woman.

                    PROSTITUTE
               (softens a bit)
          Why...thank you...sir.

               (runs a hand through his hair)
          You're a very striking man, if it's not too
          forward for me to say so.

                    CLAY

No. Not at all. Listen. I'm really rather
new at all of this, you see. I'm not sure...

PROSTITUTE
(puts finger to his lips)
Then you need little Vera's guided tour,
dear.

VERA leads him away to her bordello still
concentrating on swinging her hips as though
they're tied to a leash pulling him along.

EXT BORDELLO SAME NIGHT
Several women stand or sit on the steps. Many
men and women enter and leave the building, a
large brick house that appears to have been an
early version of a mansion. VERA leads CLAY up
the steps and through the front door.

INT BORDELLO ENTRANCE HALL SAME
NIGHT
VERA waves to her MADAM, who seems
somewhat surprised VERA has a guest. The
MADAM, a tiny woman with very thin features,
shouts out a room number above the din of
music and laughter. CLAY tries to watch all the
commotion in the adjacent rooms, but VERA
hurriedly leads him upstairs still keeping up the
hip-swing.

INT BORDELLO BEDROOM SAME NIGHT
The room is decorated in frills and bright colors.
A Virgin Mary statuette sits on the mantle. A
crucifix hangs on the wall above the bed. VERA
leads CLAY to the bed and begins undressing
him and herself. He tries stopping her several
times, but she doesn't understand and persists.
Finally, when she's down to basics, but he's still

mostly dressed, he sits abruptly on the bed and covers his face. Puzzled, she sits next to him and pulls his hands away from his face.

                    VERA
                  (shocked)
Why, you're crying. It's okay, honey, there's no need to cry about it.

                    CLAY
You don't understand.

                    VERA
Why, sure I do. I'm touched by it, really. I've never had a man cry when I've undressed in front of him before.

           (cups his chin in her palm)
Is this your first time?

CLAY begins laughing. He pats VERA's leg, then realizes it's bare and gets up to drape the coverlet of the bed around VERA's body.

                    CLAY
You don't understand, Vera. I'm...I'm not...that kind of man.

                    VERA
How many kinds of men are there?

                    CLAY
I thought I could. I really thought I could. But I can't.

                    VERA
                  (income vanishing)
Ain't I pretty enough?

CLAY hugs her, laughing. She's startled, looks around puzzled, and finally hugs him back, catching his laughter.

CLAY
You're gorgeous, Vera.

VERA
(pulling back)
I'm not the brightest woman in the world, but I don't get it.

CLAY laughs heartily, pulls her toward him again, giving her a bear hug. She feels something sticking her in his jacket pocket and reaches in to pull out two cigars. CLAY takes one, bites off the tip, motions for VERA to do the same, and they light up off of his lighter, laughing giddily as VERA chokes on the smoke.

INT A CHEAP HOTEL ROOM MORNING
Clay wakes looking haggard, but cheerful. He gets up from his double-sized bed and crosses to the mirror hung above the washstand. The only other pieces of furniture in the room are a large wardrobe with a long bottom drawer and a chair. As he rubs his hand over his stubble and looks at himself almost in disbelief, he hears a commotion outside. He crosses to the window, which he opens and leans out.

EXT STREET BELOW HOTEL WINDOW
MORNING
This is a working district, and several delivery wagons have collided causing a traffic jam. While men yell at each other in the street over

the incident, women move quickly along the sidewalks, many carrying baskets of clothing.

CLAY is surprised to see VERA, the prostitute, carrying such a basket as she crosses the street toward his hotel.

                    CLAY
              (leaning out window)
Vera! Vera! Up here. Wait. What are you doing?

                    VERA
              (glancing up)
Mr. Wright. Is that you? Be careful, you're going to fall!

                    CLAY
              (sits on sill)
Why don't you come up to talk to me?

                    VERA
I've got work to do, dear. Mrs. Vandercleven expects her wash back this morning, and I've got to pick up her dirties, as well as get Mrs. McDevon's clear over in...

                    CLAY
Laundry? When did you start doing laundry? I thought you...

                    VERA
              (waves her hands to stop his talking)
Dear Mr. Wright...

(VERA looks around)
A woman's got to make a decent living,
you know. Enough gabbing, dear, I've
got to be going. Mrs. Vandercleven won't
wait all morning.

                    CLAY
Wait. I'll come with you.

                    VERA
Whatever for?

                    CLAY
                  (smiles)
I like your company.
                    VERA
                  (smiles)
Very well then. Come along, if you're
coming.

EXT   A MORE POSH STREET IN BOSTON
MORNING
CLAY is now carrying the basket of clothing.
VERA seems uncomfortable with this fact,
worried she'll be seen by her employer. She
directs CLAY onto a back street.

EXT   THE ALLEYWAY   SAME MORNING
CLAY sees the high fences and brick walls for the
first time, never having spent much time in
areas frequented by servants. They pass other
delivery people, making way for the milk wagon.
VERA nods and responds to greetings by others.
She nods toward a large young woman in a tight
black dress and small white apron shaking rugs
at the back of one residence.

                    VERA
See her? The vixen. She used to work the
streets like I do and now she's an
upstairs maid, of all things.

          (whispers conspiratorially)
I hear she gives it free to the master of
the house.

          (pauses dramatically)
And his son.

                    CLAY
It lets her keep her job, doesn't it?

                    VERA
The boy's only thirteen!
                    CLAY
          (smiles)
I did it with the upstairs maid once.

                    VERA
          (surprised)
You?

                    CLAY
          (nods)
Hated it. She had these huge breasts...

          (makes hand gesture of size)
and I nearly suffocated in them.

                    VERA
          (laughs)
Dear, you didn't have to put your face
there, you know.

CLAY
(laughs)
But that was the best part of the whole
thing.

VERA shakes her head after giving CLAY a look
of incredulity.

VERA
This is it, dear.

EXT REAR OF VANDERCLEVEN'S HOUSE
A large brick fence encircles the backyard.
VERA opens the gate and leads CLAY up to the
back steps. A basket sits just inside the back
screen door. VERA takes the basket of clean
clothes and exchanges it for the basket of dirty.

CLAY
You mean you don't have to talk to
anyone? You just pick up what they've
left?

VERA
Yes, dear. The household servants are
too busy running the house to take time
to talk to a washerwoman.

CLAY
(carries new basket)
What if something's stained and needs
special treatment? My valet used to see
to it that the washerwoman knew stains
needed to be removed or something
needed to be sewn.

                    VERA
        (reaches inside basket under covering
        cloth, pulling out a sheet of paper)
        See? Extra starch in the gentleman's
        shirts. And I'm to sew a new button on
        the young miss' pinafore.

                    CLAY
        Pinafore?

                    VERA
        The little overdress girls wear to protect
        their real dresses?

                    CLAY
        That has a name?

                    VERA
        Everything has a name. Don't you read
        your bible? Adam named everything.

                    CLAY
        Only the animals. I doubt Adam ever
        thought about women's clothing.

                    VERA
        He might not have named them, but I
        bet he knew how to take them off.

They laugh as they go through the back gate
and continue down the alley.

                    CLAY (CONT)
        You never told me how you got started
        as a washerwoman. Or as a...lady of the
        evening, either.

                    VERA
          Well, dear. One takes a recommendation
          from someone trustworthy, the other
          takes pluck.

EXT LOWER CLASS HOUSING AREA
AFTERNOON
CLAY and VERA each carry a basket of dirties.
CLAY observes the surroundings closely, never
having really visited this part of Boston before.
VERA is brisk and business-like as she strides
down   the   street,   occasionally   greeting
neighbors.

                 NEIGHBORWOMAN
          (Swedish; leaning over a fence gossiping)
          I see you're bringing them home with
          you now, Vera.

                    VERA
          It's not like you're thinking, Edna. He's
          just a...friend.

                  NEIGHBORMAN
          (Irish; smoking a pipe on steps)
          So, that's what you call them now, eh?
          Friends, is it?

                    VERA
          Ignore them, Clay. They've nothing
          better to do.

CLAY follows VERA up the steps of a rundown
brownstone, stopping to admire some of the
stonework above the entry.

                    CLAY
These buildings must have been quite
striking in their day.

                    VERA
Weren't we all?

INT HALLWAY OF BROWNSTONE
VERA leads CLAY through the building, past
playing children and a pair of arguing women,
to the backyard.

EXT BACKYARD OF BROWNSTONE
Other women are already washing clothes in
their own tubs with their own washboards. A
high wooden fence surrounds the yard. A fire is
situated dead center, where water boils for
washing. The clothesline dominates the yard
and is already covered with drying clothing.
Several women greet VERA.

                  FIRST WOMAN
                    (Irish)
'Bout time you got here, Vera. You've
only got so much daylight left, you
know.

                    VERA
                (sarcastically)
Yes, dear, I know.

             (cheerfully to all present)
I brought help with me today.

CLAY sets his basket down beside VERA's, then
bows graciously to the women's hoots and
cheers.

                    CLAY
          At your service, ladies.

                SECOND WOMAN
                  (German)
        Our service? That's a switch, eh, girls?

                    VERA
                  (to Clay)
          Oh, no you don't. You're mine.

                (to the women)
        The rest of you can get your own.

Laughter. CLAY helps VERA empty the basket
she carried, learning to sort clothes for washing.
He holds a small petticoat up to his front. The
women laugh harder.

                FIRST WOMAN
              (tossing him another)
        Here, deary. Try this one. It's more your
        size.

CLAY holds the full-length petticoat up to
himself. It's large, so he tries it on over his shirt
and pants. It fits baggily.
                    VERA
        It's you, dear.

            (pulls it tighter from back)
        But now it looks even better. Don't you
        think so, ladies?

The women cheer; some holler cat calls. CLAY
strokes his five o'clock shadow, looks down at
himself, and smiles.

INT CLAY'S HOTEL ROOM EVENING
CLAY, who already appears closely shaven, lathers up his face and prepares to shave again. VERA, dressed in her prostitute outfit again, is laying out clothes on his bed.

                    VERA
I was able to pinch this dress from Mizz
O'Neill's basket. I never liked her much,
so I don't rightly mind if she gets in a bit
of trouble for it.

                    CLAY
What will they do to her?

                    VERA
Oh, just dock the cost from her pay, I
reckon. Or charge her with theft and
throw her in jail.

                    CLAY
Jail? I can't let a woman go to jail just so
I can have a dress to wear.

                    VERA
I don't see why not. She'll get three
meals there, and lord knows she needs
some regular eatin', what with being
pregnant and all.

                    CLAY
She's pregnant?!

                    VERA
              (deliberately dense)
Don't you worry, dear. It'll never happen
to you.

CLAY finishes shaving. VERA helps him dress, piece by piece. Then she sits him in the chair, covers his clothes with a cloth, tucking it in at the chin. She begins to apply makeup, first a heavy base coating of something like grease paint, which she dusts liberally with powder. Then she has CLAY close his eyes, so she can apply eye liner and handmade fake eyelashes. She rouges his cheeks and applies lipstick, finishing everything off with a wig.

                    CLAY
              (indicating wig)
        Where did you get this?

                    VERA
        A woman I know dresses corpses for
        burial. Apparently, someone didn't need
        this anymore.

INT LOBBY TO HOTEL NIGHT
CLAY, almost convincingly dressed as a woman, peers down into the small, poorly lit lobby from the upper landing of the staircase. VERA peeks around him. The NIGHT CLERK sits at a smaller desk behind a large, worn and dingy desk upon which sits a tattered register and a handbell. The CLERK is clearly inebriated--his head is resting precariously on his hand, elbow resting on his little desk. An almost empty glass sits tucked into one of the handy pigeonholes lining the back wall.

CLAY quietly descends the stairs with VERA right beside him. VERA giggles as they pass the CLERK, who raises his head as though in fuzzy inquiry, then, seeing two women depart, promptly tries to get comfortable again. An

ELDERLY BLACK MAN is sweeping toward the back of the hallway, just past the stairs. He stops sweeping long enough to watch the two "women" leave. He smiles and shakes his head before he resumes sweeping.

EXT REDLIGHT DISTRICT NIGHT
CLAY, still dressed as a woman, walks with VERA along the sidewalk. While his makeup is heavier, he's dressed much more modestly than VERA and the contrast seems to gather more attention.

                    MAN
          (tips his hat politely)
          Ladies. I couldn't help noticing two such
          lovely creatures as you are. I was
          wondering...

                    VERA
          We're not interested tonight.
                    MAN
          I was only wondering if...

                    VERA
          I told you; we're not interested.

CLAY smiles, unsure what to say. The MAN takes the smile as an invitation.

                    MAN
          Perhaps you're not interested, ma'am,
          but this young lady seems to be.

          (offers elbow)
          Care to take a stroll with me,
          sweetheart?

CLAY
(his voice is noticeably deep)
No, thank you.

The MAN is startled. Looks CLAY over
carefully, then leaves hastily. VERA and CLAY
laugh.

VERA
You nearly scared the poor man to
death.

CLAY
(mock feminine voice)
Pity that.

INT WOMEN'S CLOTHING STORE
MORNING
Clay, dressed as a woman, is looking at
readymade dresses. A SALESMAN waits on
him.

CLAY
(in a more believable feminine voice)
I'm really looking for something more
elegant, but modestly priced. It's my
first time...to go to the opera, you see.
And I don't want to stand out too much.

The SALESMAN shows him several pastel-
colored dresses. He chooses one.

SALESMAN
We'll have to make alterations, of
course, ma'am. Would you care to step
this way, so Mrs. Noonagan will take
your measurements.

                    CLAY
          (hands him a slip of paper)
That's not necessary. My...seamstress
uses these measurements.

                  SALESMAN
            (slightly offended)
I'm sure they would do for her, ma'am,
but we sell only quality work here, and
we'd be able to make a much better fit if
you'll allow us to take your
measurements ourselves. I'm sure you
understand.

                    CLAY
I do, I assure you. But you see I'm in
rather a hurry. And I'm sure your highly
skilled seamstress or tailor will do an
excellent job with these figures. When
will the dress be done?

                  SALESMAN
By four this afternoon, ma'am. But...

                    CLAY
That will be fine. Thank you.

INT CLAY'S HOTEL ROOM LATE
AFTERNOON
CLAY is shaving again. VERA lounges on the
bed, which is partially covered with CLAY's new
dress.

                    VERA
I hope you know what you're doing.

                    CLAY
I know.

VERA
You know what they'll do to you, if they
find out.

CLAY
What can they do to me?

VERA
Brand you a witch. Tar and feather you.
Cut off your...

CLAY
Nonsense. Many of the boys in the Army
dressed like girls for dances.

VERA
That's because they were short on real
women. There's no shortage here, dear.

CLAY
(finishes shaving)
This is the last opera of the season. I
have to go. I have to know if I am
convincing.

VERA
Why? Do you want to be a woman the
rest of your life?

CLAY
The idea has its appeal. Being a woman's
not all bad, you know.

> VERA
> (standing up)
> Not when you have a choice. If you're determined to do this pigheaded thing, let's finish it up then.

CLAY undresses, and VERA starts to dress him.

> VERA
> It's really too bad.

> CLAY
> What?

> VERA
> (stroking his bare chest)
> That this must be wasted.
> (kisses him passionately)

> CLAY
> (pushing her firmly back)
> Vera!
>
> (more gently, holding her hands)
> I love you, Vera. But not like that.

A pained look crosses VERA's face, but she continues helping CLAY dress by telling him what to do, trying not to touch him unless it's necessary. This time, she instructs him on how to apply the makeup, instead of doing it herself, taking care to stay back, touching him as little as possible.

EXT BOSTON OPERA HOUSE A WARM SPRING EVENING
CLAY, dressed as a woman (more convincingly than ever before), descends from a cab. He stops

to look at the people milling about before ascending the steps, carefully pulling up his dress as he steps. People notice the solitary woman, but aren't shocked, assuming she'll join a party. The longer CLAY dons his feminine self, the more convincing he becomes as the film progresses. Eventually, he should need little makeup or other conveyances to appear feminine.

INT ENTRYWAY TO OPERA HOUSE
Flowers adorn the entryway. CLAY stops to smell some, plucking a bloom to carry. As he smells it, he examines the people in the room to notice reactions. He smiles at those who meet his gaze. He purchases a ticket for the only class of seating available.

INT OPERA THEATER SAME NIGHT
A MAN stands to let CLAY in to his seat in the general seating on the floor. CLAY uses opera glasses to view the occupants of the boxes above, looking for friends. He spies CHARLES and TILLY who don't even seem to be communicating, although TILLY is aware of CHARLES' presence. CLAY lends his glasses to the MAN next to him, who smiles congenially at him, obviously looking him over—convinced he's a woman. Music starts and the lighting is dimmed.

INT OPERA LOBBY SAME NIGHT
Intermission. People are buying ice cream in a
cup or glasses of champagne. CLAY watches for
CHARLES and TILLY. Once he spots them, he
maneuvers his way to be near them. TILLY
notices him observing them, and assumes "she"
is ogling CHARLES, so steps between them,
blocking CLAY's view. CLAY maneuvers again,
watching CHARLES, who is chatting with
cronies, closely. CLAY, not watching where he's
going, bumps into TILLY, causing her to spill
her champagne. Everyone watches.

                    CLAY
             (patting at her dress)
         I'm so sorry, miss.

                    TILLY
             (accusingly)
         You...

             (remembering her manners)
         It's...all right. I think I can get it clean.
         I'll just visit the powder room. Maybe
         one of the matrons can help me.

                    CLAY
         Rinse it in cold water, dear.

As TILLY moves off, CLAY looks up to meet
CHARLES' eyes. CHARLES stares for several
seconds, and CLAY begins to shift expectantly,
hoping for but fearing detection. Finally,
CHARLES looks away and resumes his
conversation.

EXT OPERA HOUSE LATER THAT NIGHT
CLAY follows CHARLES and TILLY out, motioning the ATTENDANT to hail a cab. He has his DRIVER follow their carriage at a discreet distance.

EXT OSGOOD RESIDENCE SAME NIGHT
CLAY has driver stop the cab at the corner, where he can still see CHARLES and TILLY as CHARLES sees her to the door. When they embrace, CLAY leans forward as if to see better.

EXT STALLARD MANSION SAME NIGHT
Again, CLAY has the DRIVER stop a distance away. CHARLES' driver steers the carriage into the circular driveway, lets him off at the door, then drives around back. CHARLES looks around, even in the direction of the street where CLAY's carriage is parked, then disappears inside. CLAY sighs, then orders the driver on.

INT CLAY'S HOTEL ROOM NEXT DAY
CLAY lays across the bed. VERA sits in the window sill.

> VERA
> Why didn't you introduce yourself?

> CLAY
> I didn't know what to say.

> VERA
> (sarcastically)
> There's always, "Hello, how are you; won't you please fuck me?"

Their eyes meet. Both glare angrily.

                    CLAY
          You don't understand, Vera.

                    VERA
          Stop telling me I don't understand. I've
          seen lust hundreds of times, *Mister*
          Wright. I think you should forget him.

                    CLAY
          I don't have much choice, do I?

MONTAGE:
EXT BUSY STREET MORNING
It's the beginning of summer. CLAY, dressed as
a washerwoman (makeup is still noticeable),
carries a basket of clothes.

EXT ALLEYWAY SAME MORNING
CLAY dodges other delivery people as he makes
his way to a particular back yard. He enters the
gate, trades baskets, and exits, heading back the
way he came.

EXT WASHWOMEN'S YARD (VERA'S)
LATE AFTERNOON
In the same backyard as before, CLAY scrubs
clothes on a washboard in a washtub near
VERA, who does the same. He joins the chatter
occasionally but is beginning to look tired and
haggard.

EXT PARK THEATER AFTERNOON
A comic theater production plays out on a stage
in the middle of the park. Mostly lower and
lower middle class people watch, laugh, and talk
among themselves. CLAY, whose hair is
noticeably longer, is dressed as a man and sits
on a blanket on the grass next to VERA, who

looks at him longingly. He seems more relaxed, but also preoccupied.

EXT OUTSIDE MARKET DAY
VERA and CLAY, dressed as a woman, shop for groceries. She picks up a pomegranate and teases him visibly about its sexual symbolism. People begin to watch while they also try to appear oblivious.

INT A CATHOLIC CHURCH MORNING
VERA and CLAY, dressed as a woman in her Sunday best, enter. VERA dips holy water before walking down the aisle. CLAY follows. VERA kneels on one knee quickly and crosses herself before entering a pew. CLAY follows.

EXT FRONT OF VERA'S APARTMENT BUILDING EVENING
On the large sidewalk and the steps in front, VERA and CLAY, as a man, share lemonade and chat with the neighbors, washerwomen, and working class men. One of the men pours beer from his own glass mug into CLAY's lemonade (a shandy). Intrigued, CLAY sips it, likes it, and everyone laughs. Children run up and down the street, playing baseball in its earlier form.

EXT VERA'S BACKYARD LATE AFTERNOON
It's now the height of summer (the rich are out of town on vacation). The women's sleeves are rolled as high as they can get them. Some have fastened their skirts up. Few are actually washing; most lounge in the shade drinking shandies (lemonade and beer). Fewer clothes cover the lines.

INT CLAY'S HOTEL ROOM NIGHT
Finished shaving his beard, CLAY begins to shave his legs. He sets the washbasin on the floor and uses his shaving brush to stroke the suds up and down his calf. Black net stockings lie in a pile on the floor next to him.

EXT VERA'S BACKYARD EARLY AFTERNOON
CLAY enters, his basket not as full as usual. He makes an elaborate point of rolling up his sleeves (his arms aren't noticeably hairy anyway) and pinning up his skirt before he pours heated water into his tub. VERA points and jokes about his now hairless legs. CLAY throws cold water from a pitcher on her.

EXT VERA'S BACKYARD EARLY EVENING
The clothesline, which crisscrosses the yard from wooden fence to wooden fence, is empty. Most of the women are gone. VERA and CLAY lounge on the steps, sipping shandies.

> VERA
> It starts soon, doesn't it?

> CLAY
> The first ball is next month.

> VERA
> Must be nice to be rich enough to leave town when it's hot and come back to all the excitement of the social season.

> CLAY
> Yes, it was.

VERA
You'll be going back, then?

CLAY
Yes.

VERA
Why do you need those people so much?
Why can't you just go on as you have
been?

CLAY doesn't respond. He finishes his shandy, unpins his skirt, which falls around his legs as he stands. He runs his hands through his own hair, which is now long enough that he doesn't have to wear a wig. He looks around the yard, then at VERA who hasn't moved. Their eyes meet. She turns away, saddened. He picks up his basket and mounts the steps. Vera leans aside, letting him pass.

INT BALLROOM NIGHT
The room is filled almost to capacity. The August heat and the heat of bodies combine. All the women fan themselves, with the men standing near windows and doorways for relief. Many escape outside onto balconies, several of which line one side of the room.

CLAY, dressed as a woman, dances with successive men. At first, he mistakes the proper stance, trying to smile his way through his errors. Eventually, he develops a kind of rhythm and obviously begins to enjoy himself.

JOHN PAYNE, dressed in a cavalry uniform, enters, looks around, and joins some young men he knows to one side of the room. Eventually, he dances with successive women. Offering to get his current partner, TILLY, a cup of punch, he returns to discover she's talking with CLAY and CHARLES. JOHN is intrigued when this "woman" quickly persuades CHARLES to dance. JOHN watches enviously, noticing the strange quality of the attraction between the two--as though CHARLES is at once attracted and repelled by CLAY. After the dance, CLAY seeks out dance partners continuously, attempting to avoid JOHN. CLAY steps out onto an empty balcony to cool off. JOHN quickly follows.

EXT SMALL STONE BALCONY NIGHT
The view overlooks a park. Lights flicker like fireflies amongst the trees. A faint breeze ruffles CLAY's dress. Because he's sweating, his makeup is glossy and obviously heavy, so he powders his nose to try to take off the shine. JOHN pauses at the doorway, observing CLAY who faces the park, before stepping up behind him.

JOHN

It's not much cooler out here, is it?

CLAY
(startled, cornered)

No, it's not.

JOHN moves over to the other corner of the balcony. They seem to square off like boxers. CLAY is worried about his makeup melting off, but he doesn't dare touch his face because it will rub off on his gloves. He looks toward the doorway, picks up his skirts as though about to leave, then drops them, fanning himself instead.

                    JOHN
I don't remember seeing you before.
And I used to come to these things often,
just after the war.

    (extends his hand, not moving)

I'm Lieutenant John Gordon Payne. And
you are?

CLAY declines the handshake, covering his face
even more with his fan.

                    CLAY
Shouldn't we be properly introduced?

                    JOHN
You are absolutely right. I beg your
pardon, ma'am. I'll find someone to
introduce us properly.

JOHN disappears inside. CLAY turns back
toward the park. He's obviously agitated,
alternately opening his fan, waving it and
clicking it shut. JOHN quickly returns with
TILLY.

                    TILLY
Oh my, it's much cooler out here, isn't
it?

                    JOHN
Almost chilly.

TILLY moves over beside CLAY. JOHN steps up
close to CLAY's other side. CLAY steps back, as

though to leave, but JOHN puts his hand on CLAY's arm.

                    JOHN
Tilly, I've been trying to strike up a
conversation with this charming young
lady, but she insists on being properly
introduced first.

JOHN releases his touch. CLAY dabs his face
carefully with a powderpuff. TILLY smiles,
watching the interaction between the two with
curiosity.

                    TILLY
You two don't know each other? I could
have sworn...by the way you two...

                    CLAY
                  (unsteadily)
No, dear, I've never met this man before
in my life.

                    TILLY
                  (skeptical)
John, may I have the pleasure of
introducing you to Emma Bovary.

          (TILLY whispers to John)
She's a divorcee from New York, you
know.

                    JOHN
                  (bowing slightly)
How do you do, Miss...Bovary, is it?

                    TILLY
Isn't that exciting? Just like the woman
in the novel.

                    JOHN
Yes, quite a coincidence, isn't it?

                    CLAY
                 (to Tilly)
And...?

                    TILLY
Oh, yes. Emma, this is Lieutenant John
G. Payne of the United States Cavalry.
He's killed almost as many Indians as
Custer.

                    CLAY
(gently taking John's extended hand)
   How...intriguing.

                 (pauses)
Come to think of it, I have heard of you,
Lt. Payne. I understand you're quite a
lady killer, too.

                    TILLY
            (compulsorily shocked)
Emma.

                    JOHN
             (feigning innocence)
I assure you, Miss Bovary, your
reputation is safe with me.

             (extends his elbow)
Shall we dance? If you'll excuse us, Miss
Osgood.

CLAY takes JOHN's arm with feigned reluctance, and they disappear through the doorway.

INT BALLROOM SAME NIGHT
JOHN and CLAY dance to the "Nutcracker Suite's Final Waltz" by Tchaikovsky.

                    JOHN
         You'll excuse me if I sound practiced,
         but...I feel as though I've met you
         somewhere before.

                    CLAY
              (coquettishly)
         Perhaps you have, Lt. Payne.

                    JOHN
         (smiling conspiratorially)
         And were we...friends?

CLAY teases him with a smile as they continue to dance.

INT REFRESHMENT ROOM SAME NIGHT
JOHN brings CLAY, who is sitting on a couch, a glass of champagne. They strike cheers daintily. They continue to sit and drink and talk, gradually getting closer together and more relaxed with each other. Other couples come and go. Soon the room is mostly empty with just the two of them and another couple who sits across from each other in chairs closely drawn together on the other side of the room. JOHN sits down with yet another glass of champagne. CLAY tries to wave it off.

                    CLAY
          (his voice deeper, tipsy)
      No, no, no. I don't want any more.

                    JOHN
              (more sober)
      You know. I think I like you even more
      when you're drunk.

                    CLAY
      I am not drunk.

                    JOHN
      Maybe you should be.

INT CLAY'S HOTEL ROOM LATE NEXT
MORNING
Light streams through the unshaded window.
It's late enough that the sunlight angles in and
touches the end of the bed, hitting CLAY in the
face as he lies prostrate across the bed. He still
has makeup on, but it is messy. There is a lump
in the bed beside him, but it's not evident that
it's another person until CLAY sits up and takes
stock of the room and himself. Once he realizes
someone is there, he looks down at himself,
realizing he's nude and tries to cover himself up.
In doing so, he pulls the sheet off JOHN, who
remains asleep. Carefully, he slips out of bed,
stepping over to the mirror to examine his
makeup. He obviously has a hangover. He pulls
on the corset, as though for protection, and
hastily, but quietly, wipes off the old makeup,
shaves and begins applying new. He's almost
finished, when he realizes John is awake and
lying on his side on the bed, watching him.

                    JOHN
Good morning, Madame Bovary. Or
should I say, Mr. Wright?

                    CLAY
                 (horrified)
You know?

                    JOHN
How could I not know? Or don't you
remember last night?
                    CLAY
Last night? You mean the ball?

                    JOHN
                 (laughing)
I believe there was more than one.

JOHN stands and crosses, nude, to stand
behind CLAY, who still stands in front of the
mirror. They look at each other in the mirror.

                    JOHN
Or do you do this sort of thing only
when you're drunk?

                    CLAY
This sort of thing? You mean wear
women's clothes?

                    JOHN
 (pressing himself against Clay)
No, this sort of thing.

                    CLAY
Oh.

JOHN smiles so that CLAY, finally, smiles
back. JOHN swats CLAY on the behind as he
moves away to pull on his pants.

                    JOHN
     I knew there was something about you I
     remembered. But it's been a long time
     since grammar school.

                    CLAY
     Yes, I've changed a lot since then.
     Although I was still afraid you'd
     recognize me.
                    JOHN
                    (laughs)
     Actually, I probably would never have
     been able to remember who you were, if
     you hadn't told me.

                    CLAY
                    (rubbing his head)
     I told you?

                    JOHN
     I believe you mentioned it after the
     tenth glass of champagne. Of course, it
     was already obvious by then that you
     were no miss.

                    CLAY
     What do you mean?

                    JOHN
     The deeper you sink into the bottle, the
     deeper your voice gets.

By now, JOHN is nearly fully dressed. CLAY has
been watching him in the mirror.

JOHN (CONT)
So...did you mean what you said last
night?

CLAY stops applying makeup, turning to look
at JOHN.

CLAY
Which part? I haven't the faintest idea
what I said, to be honest.

JOHN stands, pants not completely fastened
and crosses over to CLAY again, touching the
makeup on his face, rubbing the greasy stuff on
his fingers and smelling it. He smiles.

JOHN
You said you wanted to fuck the
president.

CLAY resumes applying the makeup.

CLAY
Are you sure I didn't say he was fucked?

JOHN crosses to window and looks out, sitting
on sill.

JOHN
Maybe you did. I remember now
something about his Indian policy, how
you thought he should be held
accountable for the Lakota 38? Or
something like that.

CLAY finishes and turns to look at JOHN. He takes on decidedly feminine mannerisms and a convincing female voice.

> **CLAY**
> You're the first man who's paid attention when a woman talked politics.

JOHN stands and crosses to CLAY, inspecting the whole effect carefully.

> **JOHN**
> So you really consider yourself a woman now?

CLAY smiles smugly and traces a hand down one of JOHN's arms coquettishly.

> **CLAY**
> I've discovered, my dear Lt. Payne, that I can be anyone I want to be--Emma Bovary or Claypool Wright.

> **JOHN**
> (grimacing)
> You've got to pitch that Emma Bovary as a name. Don't people see right through that?

> **CLAY**
> I admit I thought of the name on the spur of the moment, but I discovered something about humanity, old chum. People want to believe you. It's either that, or they want to be fooled.

JOHN sits on the bed, clearly inviting CLAY to join him.

                              JOHN
                  Or they are fools. Same difference.

CLAY sits on the bed next to JOHN. They lean
close together, clearly toying with intimacy.
CLAY still speaks in a feminine voice.

                              CLAY
                  What about you? When did you start....

                              JOHN
                  Fucking men?

                              CLAY
                  I would have put it more delicately.

                              JOHN
                  What's delicate about it?

JOHN caresses CLAY. CLAY responds. They
begin undressing each other.

MONTAGE:
INT CLAY'S HOTEL ROOM NIGHT
Lights from the street expose the room. CLAY
and JOHN are asleep in the bed, lying in each
other's arms. Perspiration stands out freshly on
their faces.

INT CLAY'S HOTEL ROOM MORNING
JOHN is helping CLAY dress, tightening his
corset for him.

EXT A SHOPPING DISTRICT DAY
JOHN and CLAY, as a woman, are window
shopping. JOHN drags CLAY into a shop, and
they emerge with a new hat for CLAY.

INT A BAR EVENING
JOHN and CLAY, dressed as a man, are drinking with JOHN's military cronies. They laugh and joke with the others. They look at each other significantly, smiling as though enjoying their secret.

INT CLAY'S HOTEL ROOM MORNING
Sunlight coats the bed where JOHN and CLAY are making love.

EXT RESIDENTIAL STREET MORNING
JOHN accompanies CLAY, dressed as a washerwoman, on his rounds. CLAY carries the basket. JOHN seems bored.

EXT VERA'S BACKYARD AFTERNOON
CLAY and JOHN appear at back door and head toward CLAY's washtub. The jovial atmosphere, as the women realize the serious nature of their relationship, changes as their support swings to VERA. VERA tries not to show her hurt feelings but fails. CLAY and JOHN joke, seemingly oblivious to the women's attitudes. The women begin to leave.

> CLAY
> John, this is my good friend, Vera. She
> helped me become the woman I am
> today. Vera, this is my schoolboy chum,
> Lt. John Payne.

> VERA
> Lieutenant.

> JOHN
> Dear Vera. Clay's mentioned you often
> in the last couple of days. Believe me, I'll

be eternally grateful for what you've
done for this young man.

                    VERA
You mean woman, don't you?

                    JOHN
Man, woman, what's the difference?

                    VERA
Considerable. You know a man's out to
get you, but I used to think I could trust
a woman.

                    CLAY
And when someone contains the spirits
of both?

                    VERA
I'd say one of them needs to be
exorcised.

CLAY and JOHN look at each other. VERA
leaves.

EXT A PARK AFTERNOON
Leaves are changing color and the wind is brisk.
The sound of rustling leaves mixes with the
sounds of the city.

JOHN and Clay, dressed as a woman, sit on an
isolated bench. Clay's long hair and dress whip
in the wind, distracting him. JOHN takes his
hand, but Clay pulls it away to push his hair
from his face.

                    JOHN
What's left for you here?

CLAY
My friends, my family.

JOHN
Your friends don't want to be associated
with a suspected homosexual. And your
family has disowned you.

CLAY
What's out West? How would I make a
living? What if you decide you'd rather
be married to someone else? Or worse,
what if you get killed in some Indian
battle? What do I do if the Indians
attack?

JOHN
I thought you were the one who wants
the president to see them as human
beings, not savages?

CLAY
They still kill people from time to time.

JOHN
I know. I've seen the aftermath.

CLAY
People like us aren't supposed to marry.
No one would ever let us.

JOHN
I've yet to hear of anyone lifting a
woman's skirt to see if she's a she before
they'd let her take the vows.

CLAY looks searchingly at JOHN, who smiles and takes CLAY's hand, kissing the back of it.

INT JUSTICE OF THE PEACE'S RESIDENCE EVENING
CLAY, in the nicest dress he owns, stands next to JOHN as they exchange vows in front of the justice. Two witnesses stand to one side—the JUSTICE'S WIFE and THEIR MAID. JOHN smiles broadly before he kisses CLAY. The JUSTICE insists on his turn. CLAY awkwardly consents.

INT A PASSENGER CAR ON A TRAIN DAY
CLAY, now ELEANOR PAYNE, sits next to JOHN, who dozes. ELEANOR watches the women with their children, the businessmen reading their newspapers, etc. She opens a cloth package on her lap, taking out a sandwich wrapped in waxed paper. She unwraps and eats it as she turns to watch the terrain pass.

INT SAME TRAIN EVENING
ELEANOR sleeps against JOHN as JOHN cleans his pistol. Two other men, a businessman and an American Indian dressed in a suit with a Cherokee turban, sit across from them. The Indian watches JOHN clean his gun. The businessman watches the Indian.

INT ANOTHER TRAIN DAY
Less plush than the earlier train, the coach is spartan and dirtier. The seats are wooden, not cushioned. ELEANOR and JOHN eat apples from the cloth bag. The conductor comes through announcing Manhattan, Kansas. ELEANOR looks nervously outside. JOHN checks his pocket watch.

EXT MANHATTAN DEPOT DAY
JOHN deposits ELEANOR on a bench next to their luggage. He motions for her to wait. ELEANOR checks her makeup, discreetly, in a hand mirror. A man and a woman pass by as they go to the ticket counter. The man doffs his hat and smiles. The woman pulls him onward. ELEANOR smiles. As she looks around, observing the town, she sees a large building with a steeple sitting on the most prominent hill in the immediate area—the beginnings of Kansas State University.

EXT FLINT HILLS DAY
ELEANOR and JOHN ride horseback. ELEANOR is sidesaddle. JOHN leads a mule which carries their luggage. ELEANOR looks around anxiously.

                    ELEANOR
     Wasn't there any other route to the fort?
     Are you sure we won't be attacked by
     Indians?

                    JOHN
     The nearest hostile Indian's probably in
     the Dakota or Oklahoma territories.
     We're more likely to be attacked by
     bandits.

                    ELEANOR
     Bandits? You never mentioned anything
     about bandits.

                    JOHN
     I guess it slipped my mind.

Their horses head up a gravelly grade. Train tracks run along the top of the ridge. ELEANOR stops her horse and stares, incredulously, at the rails.

                    ELEANOR
          A train? A train runs through here? Does
          it go to Fort Riley?

JOHN pulls his horse to a halt after he's made it down the other side of the ridge and turns to look back.

                    ELEANOR (CONT)
          Why didn't we take the train?

                    JOHN
               (patting horse's neck)
          I had to pick up Cochise at the stable
          where I left him before I went on leave.

                    ELEANOR
          Your horse? I'm sitting sidesaddle,
          twisting the hell out of my back, because
          you had to pick up your horse?

                    JOHN
          Good, Clay...I mean, Eleanor. You've got
          it down.

                    ELEANOR
               (grumpy)
          Got what down?

                    JOHN
               (grinning mischievously)
          Being a woman.

JOHN whoops and kicks his horse into a fast gate, pulling the mule along, too, suitcases banging its sides, trunk swaying on top. ELEANOR grimaces and urges her horse down the grade.

EXT FORT RILEY EVENING
ELEANOR sits sidesaddle as she waits for JOHN to come out of a large limestone building. JOHN's horse (a buckskin, like the real Cochise) and mule are tied up to the hitching post. A train whistles in the near distance. Soldiers of various ethnic backgrounds, including an occasional Indian scout, come and go out of the building occasionally; most smile and nod their heads or doff their caps toward ELEANOR. Other limestone buildings dot the grounds, with dirt roads crisscrossing the green grass. A company of black soldiers drills under the command of a white officer on a parade ground in the distance.

A very young soldier (HIGGINS, about 16 years old) comes out of the building and approaches ELEANOR, saluting.

> HIGGINS
> (Australian accent)
> Mrs. Payne, ma'am. I'm Private Higgins. I've been instructed to escort you to your new quarters, ma'am.

> ELEANOR
> What about John...I mean, Lt. Payne? Isn't he coming?

> HIGGINS
> Presently, ma'am. He's got business to attend to. He says he'll be along shortly

and that I'm to see to your needs until
he arrives.

HIGGINS unties the mule and grasps
ELEANOR's horse's reins. He signals for a
private to take COCHISE.

                    ELEANOR
My needs? Where is he taking Cochise?

                    HIGGINS
Cochise, ma'am?

                    ELEANOR
Lt. Payne's horse.

                    HIGGINS
To the officers' stable, ma'am. Don't
worry. He'll see to the horse's needs.

                    ELEANOR
               (under her breath)
Well, as long as everyone's needs are
attended to.

EXT A LIMESTONE TOWNHOUSE DUSK
HIGGINS helps ELEANOR dismount and leads
her up the steps to the entrance on the left. He
opens the door for her and escorts her in.

INT THE HALLWAY OF THE TOWNHOUSE
HIGGINS lights several lamps, as ELEANOR
removes her hat and looks around.

                    HIGGINS
This here's the parlor. Over here's the
sitting room, and through there is the
kitchen. The bedrooms are upstairs.

The rooms are already furnished, although sparingly. No pictures hang on the wall, but a mirror does hang near the doorway. ELEANOR inspects herself and begins to smile.

                    HIGGINS (CONT)
          And there's a pump in the kitchen, so
          you don't need to draw water. You share
          the outhouse, of course, with the couple
          who live next door, if you'll pardon my
          bluntness, ma'am.

                    ELEANOR
          There's a couple living next door?

                    HIGGINS
          Yes, ma'am. These are the married
          officers' quarters.

                    ELEANOR
          And where do you live, Pvt. Higgins?

                    HIGGINS
          In the barracks on the other side of the
          parade grounds, ma'am.

                    ELEANOR
               (extending her hand)
          Please, call me Eleanor.

                    HIGGINS
          Oh, I couldn't do that, ma'am.

               (heading toward door)
          I'll unpack the mule and bring in your
          things, ma'am. Just let me know what

goes where, and I'll put things away, too,
if you'd like.

                    ELEANOR
Thank you, but I'm sure that won't be
necessary.

ELEANOR runs a hand along the banister as she
starts upstairs. She gets to the top and realizes
she needs light. Returning downstairs, she finds
a hurricane lamp on the side table next to the
entrance, lights it off one of the lamps on the
wall, and returns to the stairs. Meanwhile,
HIGGINS brings the luggage in and sets it near
the stairs.

                    HIGGINS
If that's all, ma'am, I'll go over to the
mess hall and bring you back something
to eat.

                    ELEANOR
That's not necessary, private.

                    HIGGINS
Captain's orders, ma'am.

                    ELEANOR
Captain? Captain who?

                    HIGGINS
Captain Payne, ma'am. He was
promoted in his absence, ma'am. He
told me he especially wanted me to see
to it you got fed.

ELEANOR
(pleased)
Really? Does that sort of thing happen
often?

HIGGINS
Well, usually the officers' wives cook
their own food, but seeings how you
don't have any food stocked up yet...

ELEANOR
No. I mean Lt....Captain Payne's
promotion.

I thought most of the regular Army
commissions were demoted after the
war since the Army reduced the number
of troops.

HIGGINS
It was, ma'am. Only, out here,
sometimes there's need of a successor.

ELEANOR
A successor?

HIGGINS
Yes, ma'am. Captain Fredericks was
killed on patrol while Lieutenant, I
mean Captain Payne was gone, ma'am.
The Colonel needed a man to fill his
boots, and Capt. Payne was the best
choice, so I'm told, ma'am. Now, if you
don't need me for a few minutes, I'll get
your dinner.

HIGGINS leaves. ELEANOR stands holding the lamp for a few moments, then heads back upstairs.

INT UPSTAIRS BEDROOM NIGHT
ELEANOR places the lamp on the nightstand after lighting the lamp on the wall. She sits on the edge of the mattress and tests it out.

                    ELEANOR
                 (to herself)
     I wonder if this was Captain Fredericks'
     bed.
                 FEMALE VOICE (OS)
                 (Spanish accent)
     No, it wasn't.

ELEANOR jumps up, startled. She turns to face the door, where a shadowy figure stands.

                    ELEANOR
     Who are you?

MARIA STRAW, a plump young woman (Mexican-American, Chicana), enters laughing.

                    MARIA
     I'm sorry. I didn't mean to startle you.

     (Rushes forward, hand outstretched)
     I'm Maria Straw, Captain Benjamin
     Straw's wife. I live next door. I came
     over to be hospitable and to see if you
     need any help moving in. I knocked, but
     I guess you didn't hear me.

ELEANOR
(recovering)
No, I didn't.

(taking MARIA's handshake)
I'm Eleanor Payne. Wife of
Lieutenant...I mean, Captain Payne. It
seems I just got used to calling him one
thing and now he's something else.

MARIA
You'll get used to it. Promotions
happened fast during the war. They're
not quite as fast out here, but there
always seems to be someone filling a gap
somewhere.

ELEANOR
(needing to do something)
Where are my manners? I should offer
you...something...shouldn't I?

MARIA
Not when you first move in, cariña. It's
my obligation to offer you something—
as a housewarming gift, so to speak. I
brought a peach cobbler. It's downstairs
on your dining table.

ELEANOR
(not used to such familiarity so quickly)
Really? How...thoughtful of you.

MARIA
We can boil a pot of tea, help ourselves
to some cobbler, and chat while we wait
for the men to return.

                    ELEANOR
        Return?

INT KITCHEN SAME NIGHT
MARIA sticks wood in the stove, under the
burner, and lights it.

ELEANOR sits at the table, while MARIA
bustles about making tea, cutting cobbler and
serving both up after she wipes down the dusty
table with water from the pump at the sink.
MARIA chatters while she works.

                    MARIA
        Yes, the Army wasn't meant for wives.
        They never give us a second thought. If
        they need the men for something, well,
        they take them, no "thank you, ma'am"s
        for the lending of your husband, either.
        No, when you marry a man in the Army,
        you might as well accept the fact you've
        married the Army.

MARIA sprinkles tea leaves in china cups and
pours in the hot water. She sets the teapot on a
trivet and puts a cosy over it to keep the water
warm.

                    ELEANOR
        Really?

                    MARIA
        Yes. I always thought the hardest thing
        would be sharing my husband with
        other women, if he saw fit, but I believe
        it's a thousand times worse to share him
        with the Army.

ELEANOR
I see.

MARIA
(patting ELEANOR's hand)
Don't worry, amiga. We'll manage. Why,
the last woman who lived here got on
real well with me. She loved to cook and
I...(laughs) love to eat.

ELEANOR
So, that's all you did? Cook and eat?

MARIA
Dios, no. We did lots of things. Why
there are two towns, Manhattan and
Junction City within riding distance for
shopping. And there's the monthly
officers' ball at the officers' club. Well,
really, it's just a dance, but they like to
think it's a ball. We officers' wives take
turns planning them and serving the
refreshments.

(serves the cobbler)
There's a lot to keep us busy.

There's a knock on the front door. ELEANOR
jumps, startled. MARIA laughs, getting up to go
answer it.

MARIA
Oh, that's probably Higgins back with
your dinner from the mess hall.

ELEANOR takes the opportunity of MARIA's
absence to look around the kitchen. She rubs her
face, realizing stubble has grown into shadow.

She gets a compact out of her purse and pats cake makeup on. After a vain attempt at coverup, she rolls her eyes and groans.

                    ELEANOR
          I wonder if there are other hairy women
          in Kansas.

INT TOWNHOUSE MASTER BEDROOM MORNING

ELEANOR is in bed asleep. She's sleeping in a long cotton nightgown, which contrasts with her more apparent beard stubble. JOHN, dusty and haggard, enters the room carrying his boots. He quietly sets them next to the chifforobe. While looking around the room, impressed with what ELEANOR has already unpacked, yet noting the partially unpacked trunk, he begins stripping, pausing to pour water from the pitcher into the wash bowl on a stand near the doorway. He washes his face and arms, then finishes stripping down to his shorts and undershirt. He tries to quietly crawl into bed next to ELEANOR, but she opens her eyes and smiles.

                    ELEANOR
          You're back. Finally. I was so worried.
          What time is it?

                    JOHN
          Just a little past eight.

                    ELEANOR
          In the morning?

                    JOHN
          Yes, dear. Now give me a kiss and let me
          get some sleep.

ELEANOR
I don't even get an explanation? Where
did you go? What did you do?

JOHN
I was out with another woman.

ELEANOR
(hitting him with a pillow)
Ha, ha. Where were you really?

JOHN
Let me sleep until noon, then I'll fill you
in on all the details of my honeymoon
adventures in Kansas.

ELEANOR gives JOHN an exasperated look.
JOHN plays innocent and helpless, making
ELEANOR laugh. She kisses him, then slips out
of bed. She pulls a dress and underthings out of
the chifforobe. She pours the water from the
washbasin into the chamber pot and pours out
more for herself. She strips, with JOHN looking
on appreciatively, down to camisole and
underpants. First, she inspects her chest hair.

ELEANOR
I wish I didn't have to shave so much so
often.

JOHN
Your chest has never been very hairy,
Clay.

ELEANOR
Eleanor. You better get used to calling
me that, or you'll slip up at the wrong
moment and give us away, you know.

JOHN
(rolling over)
Yeah, yeah.

ELEANOR
I wish there was some way to get rid of
hair. I guess I should be glad I'm not
going bald yet.

JOHN
Try pulling it out by the root.

ELEANOR
You mean plucking it?

(thinks about it)
I have heard that some women use
gauze and candle wax to get rid of their
facial hair.

JOHN
(muffled into pillow)
How does that work?

ELEANOR
I'm not certain yet, but I believe it
involves putting the hot wax on the hair,
then peeling it off.

JOHN
(muffled into pillow)
Sounds painful.

                    ELEANOR
                 (shaving face)
              That's what I thought.

                   (pause)
You know. It's really no fair that the
Army can just send you off like that.
Doesn't the Army have any chivalry in
its big bureaucratic heart?

                   (pause)
John?

ELEANOR turns to look at JOHN, who is
snoring lightly. She smiles and returns to her
shaving.

INT TOWNHOUSE KITCHEN MORNING
ELEANOR is going through the cupboards,
taking stock of pots and pans. The door which
leads into the backyard is open, with a screen
door to keep out insects. The one window which
faces out back is open, too. There is a knock on
the back screen door. ELEANOR looks out the
window.

                    ELEANOR
              Maria. How good to see you. Please
              come in.

MARIA enters carrying a light wooden box of
groceries.

                     MARIA
              Good morning, Eleanor. I brought you a
              little housewarming gift.

ELEANOR
But you brought me one last night.

MARIA
Oh, that little cobbler? That was only
something to fill your travel empty
stomach. This is much more practical.
Baking supplies and goods for your
larder.

ELEANOR
That's very generous of you. Thank you.

MARIA
(pleased with the reception)
De nada. You're welcome.

(helps ELEANOR put things away)

MARIA (CONT)
You know, Eleanor, I know I've only
known you a short while, but I already
feel as though I've known you forever.
As though you're the sister I never had.

ELEANOR smiles tentatively, looking guiltily at
the supplies in her hands before she continues
putting things away.

INT STRAWS' DINING ROOM EVENING
ELEANOR and JOHN sit across from each other
at the dining table, with BEN and MARIA at
either end of the table. MARIA has gone all out
on the meal, serving a roast, several vegetables,
mashed potatoes, gravy, several kinds of bread,
all of which are spread on the fairly large table
between its occupants, so that the basket of
wildflowers and two candles, the only light in

the room, seem crowded in the middle. BEN id a young, Black Irishman (which means he's Irish with Spanish blood) who is already losing his hair, has a full dark beard and mustache, which stand out against his pale face. In contrast to MARIA, he is tall and slender.

                    BEN
              (swirling his wine)
    Well, mother, you've outdone yourself
    again.

                  ELEANOR
                  (to Ben)
    Mother?

                    JOHN
    Yes, MARIA, these were quite
    sumptuous eats.

                  ELEANOR
                (to MARIA)
    Mother?

                   MARIA
            (beaming at the praise)
    I'm glad you enjoyed the meal.

              (whispers to ELEANOR)
    It's just a pet name he calls me. He says
    I remind him of his mother. Except, I
    think, she was a better cook.

                    JOHN
    Aren't mothers always?

ELEANOR
(dryly)
You've never eaten my mother's cooking.

Everyone laughs. JOHN and BEN finish their wine. MARIA gets up to get the coffee. ELEANOR gets up to assist.

JOHN
This is a tasty port, Straw. Where'd you chance upon it?

BEN
Bought it over in Junction City. A grocer over there imports a nice stock of wines and liquors. I think a good wine makes a meal more...digestible.

JOHN
(laughing)
And the company prettier?

BEN
(leaning back, smiling)
Oh, I wouldn't have Maria change one bit. She's everything I need in a woman...very carnosa.

(BEN signs "large breasts")
Your being a newlywed, I'd think Eleanor would be enough woman for you.

JOHN
Indeed.

The women return with a chocolate cake and coffee. ELEANOR pours the coffee, while

MARIA, occasionally licking the frosting with enjoyment, cuts and serves the cake.

                    BEN
          I hear you have an audience with the
          queen tomorrow.

                    JOHN
          The queen?

                    ELEANOR
          Is she really as...bad as Maria says?

                    JOHN
          She who? Bad how?

                    MARIA
          You'll see I'm not exaggerating.

                    BEN
          Your wife has been summoned by the
          Lieutenant Colonel's wife for an
          inspection.

                    JOHN
          Custer's wife?

                    BEN
          Elizabeth I'll-bring-home-the-Bacon-
          myself Custer.

                    MARIA
          Ben, querido. You really shouldn't talk
          about her that way.

                    BEN
          Why not? She thinks she's more of a
          man than her husband, although she'd

never admit she thinks that. But the way
she pushes and promotes him herself,
just so she seems to be somebody, you'd
think...

                    MARIA
Ben, please.

                     BEN
Alright. Just don't say I didn't warn you,
Eleanor. Better spit shine your shoes
and polish your buttons is all I've got to
say.

INT PAYNE BEDROOM MORNING
The bed is made, and ELEANOR is almost
finished dressing. JOHN is gone. ELEANOR
hears a knock on the door.

                 MARIA (OS)
You hoo! It's me. Are you ready?

ELEANOR grabs a cloth handbag by its string
ties, takes one last look at herself and starts
downstairs.

                  ELEANOR
I'm coming, Maria.

EXT FRONT PORCH OF TOWNHOUSE
SAME MORNING
ELEANOR comes out the door, quietly closing
the screen door behind her. MARIA is standing
at the rail surrounding the porch, watching
soldiers drilling on the nearby parade grounds.
A group of Indians, several women, one old man
and several children walk by. The women are
dressed in cheery calicos and carry woven bags

of foodstuffs. The little girls are dressed like
their mothers. The old man and the boys wear
calico shirts and jeans. ELEANOR and MARIA
watch them go by.

                    ELEANOR
          Pretty babies.

                    MARIA
          Pretty women. Are you nervous?

                    ELEANOR
          Should I be?

                    MARIA
          I was. But then I'd heard about her
          before from other officer wives at other
          posts.

                    ELEANOR
          She's that talked about?

MARIA smiles wisely, looking sideways at
ELEANOR.

                    MARIA
          Ambitious women are always subjects
          for discussion. Especially by other
          women.

EXT FORT RILEY STREET SAME
MORNING
A cavalry company with Indian scouts ride by as
ELEANOR and MARIA walk along the narrow
dirt road to where it joins a broader street. Here,
there are stately brick houses set back on plush,
well-tended lawns. Piano music drifts down
from the Custer house.

                    ELEANOR
                   (impressed)
Are you sure we're still in Kansas?

                    MARIA
That's their house down there. The
second one from the end.

                    ELEANOR
Who lives in the one on the end?

                    MARIA
That's the commander's house. The
colonel and his wife live there.

                    ELEANOR
Colonel Brown's? Why hasn't his wife
asked to see me?

                    MARIA
Officers' wives are ranked just like their
husbands. It's the second in command's
duty to see to trivial details like seeing to
new officers, so it's the second wife in
command's duty to test new officers'
wives.

                    ELEANOR
Test the wives? What kind of testing?

                    MARIA
                   (shrugs)
I don't know the wheres and the
whyfors. I'm sure this system has been
around as long as soldiers' wives have
been. But, well, it's to make sure you
understand the pecking order around

here and aren't the kind of woman
who'd try to step out of line.

                    ELEANOR
Pecking order? 'm not sure I enjoy being
likened to a chicken.

                    MARIA
                    (laughs)
What do you mean? Men have been
categorizing the kind of bird you are
since you were born, amiga. Where have
you been?

                    ELEANOR
Living like a man, I guess.

MARIA looks at ELEANOR sideways to see how
to take the joke, then laughs. ELEANOR takes a
deep breath, lifts one edge of her skirt and starts
up the walk to the Custer house. MARIA follows
one step behind.

INT CUSTER PARLOR SAME MORNING
A EuroAmerican MAID shows ELEANOR and
MARIA into the room. ELIZABETH (LIBBIE)
CUSTER, a small woman with a tiny waist, but a
self-assured air about her, sits at the piano
playing and singing "Carry Me Back to Ole
Virginny." Three other women are already
seated on the horsehair sofa and two are in
horsehair chairs (other than MARIA, none come
from an obvious ethnic background other than
Old World European). While one woman softly
sings along, the rest pretend rapt attention.

ELEANOR and MARIA are shown to leather
covered Victorian chairs as LIBBY continues to

play. One of the women on the couch leans toward the one in the middle and whispers in her ear The middle woman passes the message on to the woman on the other end of the couch (who is the one singing), who leans forward and nods in agreement toward the woman on the opposite end. MARIA and ELEANOR exchange looks, then MARIA leans in toward ELEANOR, who is removing her gloves.

                    MARIA
                 (whispers)
          The women on the couch are all majors'
          wives. They're next in importance
          behind Mrs. Custer. The other two
          women are lieutenants.

LIBBY CUSTER finishes playing with flair. The women on the couch are quick to gently applaud; the others follow suit. LIBBY rises and bows with a grandiose sweep of her hands.

                 1ST MAJOR WIFE
          Brava, brava, Libby. Your playing is
          wonderful, as always.

                 2ND MAJOR WIFE
          Yes, Libby. That piece was divine. Did
          Autie bring the music back from
          Washington on his last trip?

LIBBY picks up a fan and fans herself before sitting in a high-backed leather chair.

                    LIBBY
          Oh, dear, no. Autie's always too busy
          when he's on Army business to browse
          through music shops.

                    1ST LIEUTENANT WIFE
                        (excitedly)
          Oh, but I heard he saw Maggie Mitchell
          in *Little Barefoot* at the Palace Theater.
          A front row seat, even.

Because they aren't sure how LIBBY handles the
rumors of her husband's infidelity, two of the
majors' wives look at each other significantly,
while the third glares at the thoughtless
lieutenant's wife. MARIA senses it's time to
change the subject and stands.

                         MARIA
          Libby, I'd like you to meet Captain
          Payne's bride, Eleanor.

LIBBY stands and crosses over to ELEANOR
before ELEANOR can stand. LIBBY is so short
that she sees nearly eye to eye with seated
ELEANOR anyway. LIBBY takes ELEANOR's
gloved hand and looks her right in the eye for a
moment before she speaks.

                         LIBBY
          Eleanor, I'm delighted to meet you.
          You're from Boston, I hear. I've never
          been there, so you must tell me all about
          it sometime.

             (looks at ELEANOR's hands)
          My, what long fingers you have, dear. Do
          you play the piano, too?

ELEANOR looks at LIBBY and is disconcerted
by her direct eye contact. She turns and looks at
MARIA, who smiles encouragingly. She turns

and looks around the room at the other women,
who wait expectantly.

                    ELEANOR
     (retrieving her hand as gently as possible)
        No, I'm afraid I don't, Mrs. Custer.

                     LIBBY
        Please, call me Libby. And I hope I may
        call you Eleanor.

LIBBY smiles a practiced smile and turns to the
other women as though taking another bow. She
steps over to a table and rings a bell. A tall, thin
African American woman, ELIZA, appears with
a tray heaped with hors d'oeurves, which she
hands to LIBBY.

                     LIBBY
        Thank you, Eliza. They look splendid.
        Did you save some for the General?

                     ELIZA
        Yes, ma'am. I saved him a dozen, as you
        told me to. Should I save him some of
        the punch, too?

                     LIBBY
        No, I don't think he'd find it stout
        enough. You can serve it any time.

ELIZA prepares to leave after giving LIBBY a
short nod, taking the time to look at the women
gathered in the room. She stares at ELEANOR
the longest.

ELEANOR smiles uncomfortably, touching her
chin to feel for possible stubble.

LIBBY (CONT)
Help yourselves, ladies; we don't stand
on ceremony around here.

LIBBY passes the tray around, with each woman
taking just one hors d'oeuvre daintily.

1ST MAJOR WIFE
These are delicious, Libby. Eliza is
certainly a blessing, isn't she?

2ND MAJOR WIFE
Indeed. Where did she learn to make
them so...moist?

ELEANOR is having problems eating hers. She
leans toward MARIA as the other women
continue to chatter. She's surprised MARIA has
already eaten hers.

ELEANOR
(whispering)
How can you eat this? It tastes
like...like...I don't know what. What is
it?

MARIA
A sort of pate, I guess. I thought it
was...all right. What's wrong with yours?

ELEANOR shrugs and stuffs the hors d'oeuvre
in her mouth, swallowing with some difficulty.
ELIZA returns with the punch and ELEANOR
eagerly drinks hers. The other women look on in
mild amazement.

LIBBY
Do you hunt, Eleanor?

                    ELEANOR
              (clears her throat)
Hunt?

                    LIBBY
Yes, fox hunt. Ride with the hounds?

                    ELEANOR
Yes, once or twice, in England, actually.
But...

                    LIBBY
But what, dear?

                    ELEANOR
There's fox hunting here?

                    LIBBY
Yes, the General takes us out with his
hounds, Rover, Butcher, Otto and the
others, to break the monotony on
occasion. Would you care to join us
sometime?

                    ELEANOR
Well, yes, except...

                    LIBBY
Except?

                    ELEANOR
I've never hunted sidesaddle before, and
I'm afraid my husband won't let me ride
any other way now.

LIBBY laughs and the other women follow suit.

LIBBY
I'm surprised that the English, who
seem so refined, would allow a woman
to hunt astride. I'm afraid I'll have to
side with your husband, Eleanor. But
don't worry, it's safe enough here on the
prairie.

ELEANOR smiles tentatively and looks at
MARIA, who sips her punch.

ELEANOR
Mrs. Custer, I mean Libby, I don't want
to appear ignorant, but I'm afraid I'm
rather new at all of this. Who is the
General?

LIBBY
Why, General Custer, of course.

The women all laugh again.

INT THE PAYNE BEDROOM EVENING
JOHN is laughing heartily as he lies, at ease, on
the bed, boots off, with his upper body leaning
against the headboard, propped up by pillows.
ELEANOR is pacing the room, occasionally
stopping to lean on one of the posts at the foot
of the bed.

ELEANOR
Go ahead, laugh. You never told me it'd
be like this.

JOHN
What was to tell?

ELEANOR
Tea parties? Pecking orders, servants,
fox hunting, predatory women, awful
hors d'oeuvres. No. You let me worry
about Indians, a peaceable people who
are hundreds of miles away, but you
didn't tell me about the real dangers.

JOHN
You're the one who had the dime novel
ideas about the West, remember? I
learned a long time ago that telling
people back East what life was really like
here would either lead them to think me
a liar or entice them out here. And, as
far as I'm concerned, it's too crowded
here already.

ELEANOR
Crowded is right. I've never felt so
confined before. But fox hunting? In a
spine breaking sidesaddle?

JOHN
Believe me, I've been on several of these
little excursions with Custer. The
hounds always outpace us and we,
officers and gentlemen that we are, hang
back and ride with the ladies. It's more
of a social event, not a real hunt.

ELEANOR
Do I have to address Custer as General
or as Lt. Colonel?

JOHN
Only Custer, Libby, and his servants call
him General. He might still consider

himself a Civil War general, but he's only drawing Lt. Colonel pay.

                    ELEANOR
                (sits beside JOHN)
This is all a little overwhelming. I thought we'd be more...alone. That I'd keep house, bake cakes and roast chickens, and you'd do whatever it is you do, come home, eat the meals I so lovingly produced, then spend the rest of the time with me.

                     JOHN
We're alone now.

ELEANOR smiles knowingly. JOHN smiles back. They kiss.

EXT   PARADE GROUNDS   EARLY MORNING
ELEANOR and JOHN, dressed for fox hunting, she in the only suit she brought, he in a more casual, but still military uniform, sit astride their horses. Two of the majors' wives and one lieutenant's wife, and their husbands, are also mounted and waiting. Several single officers, many who imitate CUSTER's typical attire with buckskin pants and large Bolero hat, and one INDIAN SCOUT fill out the hunting party. Dogs are barking in the background. Everyone turns to look where the sound comes from. LIBBY, smartly decked out, sits astride her mount as it ambles toward the group. An African American man, the HOUNDS KEEPER, holds onto the leashes of several staghounds and beagles as they drag him across the grounds behind LIBBY.

JOHN
(to ELEANOR)
Ben is officer of the day, so he won't be
here. Maria doesn't hunt?

ELEANOR
No, she's afraid she'd break a horse's
back jumping over a fence.

JOHN
There are very few fences out here.

LIBBY reins her horse to a halt. The other horses
stir because of the proximity of the barking
dogs.

LIBBY
The General asked me to send his apologies. He
was suddenly called away to Washington
yesterday, but wanted us to go ahead and enjoy
ourselves, gladly giving us loan of his dogs.

FIRST MAJOR
(Swedish)
That was very generous of him, Mrs.
Custer. But, if you'd rather not go
without him, I'm sure we'll all
understand.

LIBBY
Oh, no! I insist and fully plan to
participate with vigor, myself. Besides, a
couple of the professors from the
university over in Manhattan plan to
meet us near the Konza River. I wouldn't
want to disappoint them. Shall we go?

The HOUNDS KEEPER releases the dogs, who start off eagerly toward the eastern edge of the fort's land. The party of riders follows along at a walk, then a trot, chatting amiably.

EXT   PRAIRIE   MORNING
The hounds are chasing a coyote which lopes over rise after rise almost as if leading the dogs on deliberately. After the hounds pass, still following the coyote, the riders come into view, LIBBY and several of the single officers lead the way. JOHN is ahead, then drops back to check on ELEANOR, who is trying to bear the sidesaddle gracefully.

JOHN
(loping his horse beside ELEANOR's)
How are you?

ELEANOR
(through gritted teeth, but smiling forcibly)
Lovely. Just lovely.

From the right, a group of riders, three men and a woman, also outfitted for hunting, race toward the hunting party.

JOHN
Must be the university people.

LIBBY and several others stop their horses, while the rest race on after the hounds. ELEANOR waves JOHN on and pulls up beside the stopped group. No one takes particular notice of her, except NEISMAN, now a professor at the university.

                    LIBBY
...couldn't come, but we're so delighted
you found us.

              FIRST MALE RIDER
Well, you're a bit off from where we said
we'd meet, but we heard the hounds and
knew where to find you.

                    LIBBY
Excellent. Shall we continue the pursuit,
then?

Most of the group follows LIBBY onward.
ELEANOR groans and rubs her back and
watches them go on. One of the new riders,
PROF. NEISMAN, comes up to her, pulling up
alongside her horse.

                  NEISMAN
Are you all right, ma'am?

                  ELEANOR
                 (startled)
Yes, I...it's just my back. I'm not used to
riding sidesaddle so much.

ELEANOR recognizes the slightly older
NEISMAN, but she isn't panicked that he
might recognize her. She's amused, in fact, that
he doesn't.

                  NEISMAN
Perhaps if I...rub it for you?

NEISMAN sidles up closer and reaches over to
rub ELEANOR's back. ELEANOR watches his
face carefully for a sign of recognition.

ELEANOR
Why, professor, do you give back rubs
like this to all the women in sidesaddle?

NEISMAN
(smiling lecherously)
Only when they need it.

(NEISMAN gives one last rub)
I think we'd better catch up to the rest of
the group, Miss....

ELEANOR
Mrs.... Mrs. John Payne. And you are?

NEISMAN
Prof. Edward Neisman, at your service,
Mrs. Payne.

ELEANOR
(coquettishly)
I'll have to remember that, Prof.
Neisman.

ELEANOR kicks her horse into a lope.
NEISMAN follows suit, catching up with her
quickly. ELEANOR, with a mischievous grin on
her face, kicks her horse harder. NEISMAN
gives chase.

INT   PAYNE KITCHEN   EARLY EVENING
MARIA is fixing dinner, occasionally adding a
stick of wood to the stove as she works.
ELEANOR peels potatoes. MARIA keeps
glancing at ELEANOR, who is deep in reverie.

MARIA
You know, ever since you returned from
the hunt, you've been positively stoney.
Yet there's this little glow about you, too.
You're not pregnant, are you?

ELEANOR
Pregnant, me? Oh dear, no.

MARIA
How can you be so sure? Are you having
your monthly flow?

ELEANOR
(hoping to silence MARIA)
Maria, really. Such talk in the kitchen?

MARIA
Where else would be more appropriate?
You know, you shouldn't be handling
food if you are...you know.

ELEANOR
No, I don't know. What on earth are you
talking about?

MARIA
They must raise girls differently in
Boston, is all I've got to say. You mean
your mother didn't warn you you could
die if you touched water when your
period was on? Or that you'll
contaminate food

(MARIA takes away the potatoes)
with your menstrual odors?

                    ELEANOR
Don't be ridiculous.

          (takes potatoes back)
Now let me finish this in peace, will you?
I swear, you're worse than a mother hen.

                    MARIA
See, even you're talking chickens now.

EXT   PAYNE/STRAW BACKYARD
MORNING
Bright sunshine, blue skies and a light breeze
reveal ELEANOR shooing several chickens
away from her wash line, then finishing hanging
up her wash, which dances gently in the early
autumn air. As she pours out the remainder of
her wash water, MARIA comes out with a basket
load of clothes.

                    MARIA
Up with the chickens this morning, I
see.

                    ELEANOR
Speaking of chickens, isn't there any way
to keep these penned up, so they don't
do their business all over the yard?

                    MARIA
Pen up a chicken? That would ruin the
quality of the eggs.

          (pours water into tub)
You do like fresh eggs, don't you?

ELEANOR
Yes, but these are your chickens. Isn't
there some way you can keep them on
your side of the yard?

MARIA
(offended)
Haven't I shared the eggs, not to
mention heaps of other food, with you?

ELEANOR
Well, yes, but...

MARIA
(near tears)
Are you saying you want to end our
friendship just because of some
chickens?
ELEANOR
(defensive)
No, that's not what I meant at all.

MARIA
(suspicious)
Are you going to see Libby today?

ELEANOR
Well, yes, aren't you? Weren't you
invited to tea this afternoon?

MARIA busies herself with hanging her
laundry, trying to recover her dignity.

MARIA
No, I wasn't.

ELEANOR
I'm sorry.

                    MARIA
Don't be. It's not your fault.

                   ELEANOR
I didn't know her friendship meant so
much to you.

                    MARIA
Libby isn't anyone's friend, but it doesn't
reflect well on...Ben, if she doesn't invite
me.

                   ELEANOR
I had no idea she had such influence.

                    MARIA
Any woman worth her salt influences
her husband's decisions.

                   ELEANOR
                  (laughing)
Surely, you're not as serious as you
sound. A man will make his own
decisions regardless of what his wife
thinks. Especially when it comes to
business.

                    MARIA
                  (smiling)
You're still a newlywed yet.

                   ELEANOR
So?

MARIA

Eleanor. Unless he's a brute, a man
won't force himself on you if you say no.
The longer you say no, the more
influence you wield.

ELEANOR
(amused)

Maria. I had no idea you were such a
conniving woman.

MARIA

Aren't you?

ELEANOR shakes her head, semi-seriously. She picks up her empty basket and waves back to MARIA as she enters the house.

INT   CUSTER PARLOR   AFTERNOON
LIBBY sits in her highbacked chair. She's in an elaborate white dress with a matching spray of baby's breath in her pinned up hair. Two of the majors' wives sit on the sofa. ELEANOR sits in a chair near the window, opposite LIBBY. All four women hold tea cups and saucers, with little crispy cookies lining the edges of their saucers. A tray of such goodies sits beside the tea pot on the center table. No one is saying anything. ELEANOR bites from a cookie and has some trouble getting the crumbs off her face, but she manages. The other women sip their tea occasionally.

ELEANOR

These biscuits are quite tasty, Libby.

LIBBY
(as though in reverie)
Biscuits?

FIRST MAJOR WIFE
I believe she means the cookies, dear.

LIBBY
Oh yes, the cookies. Thank you, Eleanor.
Eliza made them especially for today.

SECOND MAJOR WIFE
I must get the recipe for them.

LIBBY
I'm sure Eliza would be flattered.

The ensuing silence hangs heavy. ELEANOR
shifts uncomfortably.

ELEANOR
(clearing her throat)
I don't mean to pry, Libby, but...

Everyone turns to look at ELEANOR
suspiciously.
ELEANOR (CONT)
I'm sorry. I don't know what else to do.

LIBBY
(almost impatiently)
What is it, Eleanor?

ELEANOR
I've noticed that you seem...

Everyone stares even more intently.

ELEANOR (CONT)
...rather preoccupied. Is there
something wrong?

LIBBY lets out a big sigh and puts the back of
her hand to her mouth rather melodramatically.
The majors' wives look put out with ELEANOR.
ELIZA comes to the doorway. She takes time to
survey the room and its occupants before
speaking.

ELIZA
Mrs. Custer, there's a gentleman caller
here. He says he's from the university.
Rode in the hunt with you the other day.
He's come to pay his respects.

LIBBY
Show him in, Eliza. And bring us a fresh
pot of tea.

ELIZA nods, looks ELEANOR in the eye, and
retreats. LIBBY tries to perk herself up by going
to the piano.

LIBBY
Let's show the professor how gay we can
be, shall we?

LIBBY begins playing and singing "In the
Gloaming" by Annie Fortescue Harrison. ELISA
returns with Prof. NEISMAN, who is dressed as
he was for the hunt, carrying his hat in his hand.
He nods to the majors' wives first, then to
ELEANOR. He pauses while making eye contact
with her to smile lasciviously at her. She notices
the majors' wives noticing and shifts
uncomfortably but offers her only gloved hand

(carefully holding her teacup in the other) to the professor, who kisses it a little too long. LIBBY stops in the middle of the song, noticing, too. Everyone looks at LIBBY. The professor gallantly bows toward the piano.

                    NEISMAN
          Ah, Mrs. Custer. You look so radiant
          today. Almost as if you were fresh from
          the hunt.

                    LIBBY
          You're looking rather fresh yourself,
          Prof. Neisman. Ladies, you've all had the
          pleasure of making Prof. Neisman's
          acquaintance, I assume.

LIBBY looks significantly at ELEANOR. ELEANOR straightens her spine and looks her back in the eye. She speaks in a lustily deep voice.

                    ELEANOR
          Yes, Libby. I've had that honor.

Prof. NEISMAN smiles, sensing a minor squabble over him. He sits in a chair close to ELEANOR.

                    NEISMAN
          I understand the General was called to
          Washington rather suddenly, Mrs.
          Custer. I'll never understand how any
          man could ever leave your side for more
          than a few minutes.

LIBBY beams triumphantly, moving from the piano to NEISMAN's side. Taking his hand, she pulls him to his feet.

                    LIBBY
          You flatter me, Professor. Have I ever
          shown you my husband's prized
          collection of books?

She begins to lead him out of the parlor, then remembers her other guests.

                    LIBBY (CONT)
          Eleanor, I don't believe I've had the
          chance to show you either. Will you two
          ladies entertain yourselves, while the
          three of us dash upstairs to peek at the
          library.

The majors' wives are a bit put out but continue to sit on the sofa. ELEANOR sets her cup and saucer down and follows LIBBY and NEISMAN out.

INT UPSTAIRS HALLWAY OF CUSTER HOUSE
LIBBY is still leading the professor by the hand. He looks back at ELEANOR and shrugs once while LIBBY chatters.

                    LIBBY
          Being a man of letters, I'm sure you'll
          find the collection miniscule, but
          immaculate. Autie would be honored to
          know you took the time to examine it,
          though, Prof. Neisman.

NEISMAN
The honor's all mine, I'm sure.

INT CUSTER LIBRARY
LIBBY leads them into a small corner room. On each of two sides, large two pane windows look out onto trees whose leaves are falling. Opposite the windows, two walls have large bookcases built into the walls. The cases are filled, but not full, with various adornments, like figure busts, filling in gaps. A fairly large wooden desk and leather chair sit catty-corner, so that the chair's occupant can see out either window. Several papers are neatly stacked to one side. An elaborate pen holder sits at the top of the desk. A small red book sits in the center of the large paper blotter covering the desktop.

NEISMAN approaches the bookcases and begins reading spines. LIBBY watches him, hoping for a sign of pleasure. ELEANOR moves silently toward the windows and peers out. As she watches LIBBY dote on NEISMAN, she crosses to the desk and picks up the book on the blotter. Its spine says JOURNAL in gold lettering. She looks up to see if LIBBY or NEISMAN notices, then opens the cover of the book. The inside leaf says, in a floral script, "The personal diary of Elizabeth Bacon Custer." ELEANOR is startled when NEISMAN clears his throat.

NEISMAN
(looking in ELEANOR's direction)
As I was saying, Mrs. Custer...

LIBBY
Oh, please, professor, call me Libby.

NEISMAN
It would be an honor...Libby.

(looks toward ELEANOR)
As I was saying, Libby, this is a fine
collection of books. Did you help the
General put it together?

LIBBY
Well, I...I don't want to seem immodest,
but...yes, I chose several of these for
him. Bought several for him,
myself....professor.

NEISMAN
I must commend you on your
impeccable taste, Libby. Please, call me
Edward.

LIBBY
Thank you....

(with emphasis)
Edward.

NEISMAN
(turning to face ELEANOR)
And you, too, Mrs. Payne. I would
consider it an honor if you would be so
kind as to consider me enough of
a...friend to call me, Edward, as well.

LIBBY steps back, watching ELEANOR and
NEISMAN's friendly, familiar interaction.

INT   PAYNE BEDROOM   NIGHT
Through the window, a half-moon shines across beds of fallen leaves and half-nude trees. The moonlight stretches across the floor and over the bed, where JOHN and ELEANOR are making love. JOHN is amorous, ELEANOR less receptive. Finally, JOHN lies back and sits up against the headboard.

                    JOHN
          You're not in the mood tonight.

                    ELEANOR
          Sorry.

                    JOHN
          (turning the bedside lamp up)
          You seem really preoccupied. Is
          something bothering you?

                    ELEANOR
          No...no...I'm just...tired.

                    JOHN
          Living in the wild west is getting to you?

                    ELEANOR
          Wild West. It can't be too wild if there
          are universities with professors out here.
                    JOHN
          You still thinking about your encounter
          with Neisman at the hunt?

                    ELEANOR
          I encountered him again today.

                    JOHN
Oh? Been sneaking off to Manhattan
behind my back? Was it as good as you
remembered?

                  ELEANOR
                 (grimacing)
Don't be cruel. I saw him at the Custers'.

                    JOHN
Oh, yeah. Ben mentioned Maria got the
brush-off today. I told him not to worry.
The real man of the house has gone to
Washington.

                  ELEANOR
            (rolling her eyes at him)
You're as bad as the rest. Libby, despite
her need for adulation, isn't a bad
person. I think she's really very lonely,
especially since her husband seems to
prance around on her frequently.

                    JOHN
                  (mocking)
Prance around on her?

                  ELEANOR
You know what I mean. He's got some
woman back in Washington.

JOHN
Yeah, she's called the U.S. Army.

ELEANOR
No, I'm serious. She's an actress or
something.

JOHN
I know. I've heard the rumors. I just
think you're taking Mrs. Custer's
problems too seriously.

JOHN gets up and goes to the dresser, picking
up a cigar. He bites off the end and lights it.

ELEANOR
And what if I fooled around on you?
How would that make you feel?

JOHN
You fool around on me and you're liable
to get us both hanged for illegal
fornication with

(mock ominously)
the same sex.

ELEANOR
Don't tell me that on those long tours of
duty out on the plains when you
troopers have to share beds to stay
warm that there's no shenanigans going
on. I know better.

JOHN moves over to the chair by the window,
picks up and slips on his pants.

JOHN
I'm hungry. How 'bout you?

ELEANOR
(exasperated)
John! Aren't you going to answer me?

JOHN
I didn't know you asked a question.

JOHN disappears through the doorway.

ELEANOR
(shouting)
Aren't you going to tell me?

JOHN
(shouting back)
Shh! The walls have ears.

MONTAGE:
INT   JUNCTION CITY DRY GOODS STORE
DAY
ELEANOR and MARIA are shopping. A couple of women (who will reappear later), wives of enlisted men, with several children in tow pay for their goods and leave. MARIA is looking at cloth; ELEANOR looks at books. She finds a JOURNAL like LIBBY's and picks it up, opening the book so that the spine makes a cracking sound. She turns the pages, all empty, and smiles. Closing the book, she puts it on the counter with her other purchases. The clerk puts it in a box with everything else.

INT PAYNE KITCHEN EARLY AFTERNOON
ELEANOR unpacks the groceries and dry goods from Junction City. She lingers over the Journal, rubbing its spine with her hand.

INT FIRST FLOOR HALLWAY
Carrying the Journal and humming "Hiding in Thee," ELEANOR begins to climb the stairs.

INT PAYNE LIBRARY
ELEANOR carries the Journal into the little library she has set up in a back room upstairs. A small desk with a chair sits in front of the one window facing out into the backyard where chickens are scattered. One bookcase is against the opposite wall, with about 10 books tidily lined on a shelf. She sets the Journal on the desk blotter.

INT PAYNE PARLOR MID AFTERNOON
ELEANOR is cleaning. She dusts all the knickknacks, wipes down the shelves and wooden furniture, cleans the inside of the windows. She stops to look out, watching a small group of soldiers drill on the parade grounds across the street. She rests a hand on the glass, watching it steam up the glass and smiles.

INT PAYNE KITCHEN LATE AFTERNOON
ELEANOR finishes peeling potatoes and puts a large pot of them on to boil. Drying her hands, she takes off her apron and sets it on the table.

INT PAYNE LIBRARY AFTERNOON
ELEANOR enters, turning up a lamp to the growing gloom. She looks at a small mantle

clock she has on the top of the bookcase. It's 4:45. After carefully opening a new bottle of ink, she opens the journal to the first cover leaf and picks up a quill pen. Very carefully, she writes: "The personal diary of Eleanor Payne." She blows the words dry, then presses back the page and dates the next one: "October 15, 1874." She takes a deep breath and begins to write: "What a life I'm leading." As she writes, we move back to the window.

EXT   PAYNE BACKYARD
In the backyard, through the window, we see the final leaves fall from the tree, snow fall, melt, and buds come out.

INT   PAYNE BEDROOM....LATE MORNING
ELEANOR, whose dress and general appearance has changed to reflect the passage of time, tips a candle over a saucer, allowing the wax to pour. She then takes a small piece of gauze, places it over her mustache, and proceeds to smear the hot wax over the gauze. She fans her face with a fold out fan until the wax cools and hardens. Once the wax is hard, she grips the edge of the gauze and pulls it off quickly. ELEANOR abruptly stands and covers her mouth, conscious of the tender upper lip, but stifles a scream. She then takes a handkerchief and daubs her eyes before resolutely repeating the wax treatment to her beard.

INT   PAYNE LIBRARY   AFTERNOON
Pulling back inside, ELEANOR is finishing an entry for May 15, 1875:   "Prof. Neisman is coming to tea." As she finishes writing the line, MARIA calls up to her from downstairs.

MARIA (OS)
Eleanor, the professor just pulled up in
his buggy. Should I set out the canapes?

ELEANOR
Yes. And please put the kettle on for tea?

ELEANOR closes the journal, stands and runs
her hands down her skirt, briefly touches her
hair, then leans down to peer out the back
window where chickens are scattered. She hears
a bell ring at the front door and listens for
MARIA to answer it. She steps out of the room
to the head of the stairs and peers down.

INT PAYNE PARLOR AFTERNOON
MARIA shows NEISMAN a comfortable chair,
one of a pair next to a small table. She excitedly
excuses herself just as ELEANOR steps into the
room. NEISMAN stands again, gallantly taking
ELEANOR's hand and kissing the back of it after
making sure MARIA is gone.

NEISMAN
Eleanor, you look radiant.

(looking in direction MARIA exited)
I didn't know we'd...have company
today. I was in hopes it would just be the
two of us.

ELEANOR
(offering a canape from tray on table)
Edward! How forward of you. You know
how tongues would wag if you visited me
now unchaperoned, what with John
away on a campaign and me all alone
here.

NEISMAN smiles and bites off a bit of the canape as though he's being sexually suggestive. ELEANOR demurely, coyly, sits in one of the chairs, setting the tray on the table. NEISMAN starts to sit in the opposite chair, but motions toward the sofa.

                    NEISMAN
          Don't you think we'd be more
          comfortable over here?

                    ELEANOR
          Comfort is something I'm not willing to
          give you, just yet, professor.

NEISMAN sits in the chair opposite ELEANOR with an almost childlike grin of glee on his face.

                    NEISMAN
          You mean that there's hope that you
          will? Soon?

MARIA enters with a pot of tea and three cups on another tray. She's overheard part of the conversation and doesn't approve, exhibiting her displeasure in a scowl. She sets the tray down on another small table in front of the sofa with much ado and noise.

                    MARIA
          I assume we're all ready for tea now.

                    ELEANOR
          Yes, Maria, we're ready.

MARIA begins pouring tea and handing out cups. As she hands NEISMAN his, she begins interrogating him.

MARIA
So, professor, how is this term going?
Any problems among your students?
Anyone caught cheating

(looks at ELEANOR)
recently?

NEISMAN
No. I'm happy to report, Mrs. Straw, that my students have been perfect angels this term.

MARIA
Is that unusual, professor?

NEISMAN
(looking at ELEANOR)
No, indeed, Mrs. Straw. I've always been known as a teacher who puts his students through their paces. They don't dare get out of line with me as their master.

ELEANOR
You make it sound as if your students are all animals, professor.

NEISMAN
Young men at this age can be, I assure you, Mrs. Payne. You're fortunate to be dealing with me, instead of them. They have absolutely no control over their baser needs.

MARIA
(between sips)
So you set an example for them, do you?

EXT FLINT HILLS AFTERNOON
ELEANOR and NEISMAN ride in his buggy on
a well-worn strip of dirt road. The afternoon is
sunny and warm. Birds sing and fly up as the
horse and buggy pass. The rolling hills are
fecund with tall green, swaying grasses and
flowers. NEISMAN steers the horse off the road
and up a knoll, pulling to a halt at the end of the
ridge. The hills roll away like lounging bodies
before them. The fort is visible three or four
miles away. They get out of the buggy and walk
a little way away.

NEISMAN
And all this could be yours, Eleanor.

ELEANOR
You're so generous. How magnanimous
of you to give me something you don't
even own.

NEISMAN
Farmers give up their homesteads all the
time. It wouldn't be much of a trick to
buy a decent plot of land to raise a few
chickens on.

ELEANOR
You expect to quit the university and try
your hand at raising chickens?

                    NEISMAN
                    (laughs)
Oh, the chickens aren't for me. They're
for you.

                    ELEANOR
And what would I want with a bunch of
chickens?

                    NEISMAN
You could collect the eggs and sell them
for some income of your own, while I do
the important things like teach.

                    ELEANOR
Oh. I see. This is your way of telling me
to leave my husband and come live with
you? How does the verse go? "Come live
with me and be my love and we will all
the pleasures prove"?

                    NEISMAN
            (putting his arm around her)
Exactly.

                    ELEANOR
Why, Professor Neisman, I could never
leave my husband.

                    NEISMAN
What's he got that I haven't got?

                (kisses her)

                    ELEANOR
I don't know. Maybe you could show me.

Entwined, and kissing passionately, they sink to the ground. NEISMAN eagerly pulls up ELEANOR's skirts and gropes upwards. He stops when he discovers something unexpected. He pulls away from kissing and looks at ELEANOR's face, then pulls up the skirt for a better look. He sits down hard and looks at ELEANOR's face again.

                    NEISMAN
          You're...you're a...

                    ELEANOR
          What's the matter, professor, has it been
          that long?

                    NEISMAN
          Has what been that long?

                    ELEANOR
          You mean you don't recognize me?

ELEANOR is genuinely surprised. She sits hastily up, instinctively pulling down her skirts.

                    ELEANOR (CONT)
          I thought you knew. I thought you were
          just playing along.

                    NEISMAN
          Playing along?

NEISMAN scrutinizes ELEANOR's face, jerking back her hair for a better look. Finally, he recognizes her, and stands, clearly agitated, continually rubbing his mouth with the back of his hand.

NEISMAN (CONT)
Oh, my god, I know you now. Wright.
Claypool Wright from Boston.

ELEANOR
Yes, it's me. Surprised?

NEISMAN begins spitting as though with a
bitter taste in his mouth. He takes out a
handkerchief and wipes his hands as though
trying to get something off of them, moving
continually further away.

NEISMAN
Oh god. I purged that...that...from me.
I...I...never wanted to do that again. And
now...now you've led me on. You almost
let me.... And now you...look at you.
You've become a fucking woman! How
could you sink this low?

ELEANOR
I don't understand. I thought you said
you would always...love men.

NEISMAN
I thought you were a woman! I...I...you
don't understand. I found God, and a
man should never lie with another man
as he does a woman. It's sinful.

ELEANOR
(laughing scornfully)
A sin? You were just about to fornicate
with another man's wife. What about
"covet not thy neighbor's wife"? Isn't
that a sin?

NEISMAN
Not as bad.

(defensively)
I might have married you...eventually.
Made an honest woman of you.

ELEANOR
Made an honest woman of me!? Noble
and decent human being that you are
you might have eventually married me
just to clear your own sinful conscience.

NEISMAN
(full implications hit him)
My god, Clay. Does Capt. Payne know?

He must. You've entered into a legal
marriage with another man? You've
committed, and probably continue to
commit, sodomy under religious and
government sanction?

ELEANOR has picked up her hat and is
marching toward the buggy. NEISMAN runs
after her.

NEISMAN
Oh, no you don't. Not in my buggy, you
son of Sodom.

As ELEANOR tries to climb into the buggy,
NEISMAN pushes her away, climbing into the
buggy himself.

NEISMAN (CONT)
You can just walk back to the fort.

ELEANOR
Don't be ridiculous.

NEISMAN whips the horse into motion,
leaving ELEANOR behind.

ELEANOR (CONT)
Wait! Edward! Wait!

NEISMAN stops, ELEANOR runs to catch up.

ELEANOR (CONT)
I knew you couldn't leave me.

NEISMAN
Oh no, you don't. I meant what I said.
Just what do you think your husband's
superiors would do to the two of you if
they knew, huh? Probably string you up
or at least tar and feather you. Maybe
they'd even horsewhip you in front of
the troops ,so no one else would get any
ideas. Don't you think?

ELEANOR
No. You wouldn't. You can't.

NEISMAN
Oh? And just why not?

ELEANOR
What would your precious university do
to you if they found out you were fired
from Harvard for sleeping with a man
you slept with again here? A man who
dresses like a woman.

NEISMAN
I haven't slept with you here.

ELEANOR
And just who would they believe? A man
who tried to seduce another man's wife
and discovered she was male? The same
man who was let go from Harvard for
unsavory practices with his students?

NEISMAN
You were the only one. I swear.

ELEANOR
Do you think that would make much
difference to them?

NEISMAN thinks over the threat. Grimaces
and shrugs.

NEISMAN
You still walk back.

NEISMAN clucks the horse on. From our
withdrawing bird's eye view: ELEANOR
watches the buggy retreat, looks around at her
isolation, then starts walking back to the fort.

When we pull back far enough, our gaze
becomes that of a SENTRY on horseback on a
nearby knoll who has apparently watched the
scenario through a pair of binoculars. He
laughs, then turns to his companion, passing off
the binoculars.

FIRST SENTRY
Looks like the professor lucked out. She
must not have been willing to give him
any.

SECOND SENTRY
Think we should go rescue her? I'm sure
Capt. Payne would be grateful.

FIRST SENTRY
Yeah, but then he'd want to know why
she was abandoned out here. I'm not the
messenger of infidelity for any man.

SECOND SENTRY
Think she'll be okay?

FIRST SENTRY
No Indians or bandits within miles.

SECOND SENTRY
Hate to see a woman treated that way.

FIRST SENTRY
From what I hear, she's more man than
woman.

SECOND SENTRY
Oh?

The FIRST SENTRY smiles broadly and takes
back his binoculars for one last look. Then he
packs them in his saddlebag and turns his horse
away. The SECOND SENTRY shades his eyes
and tries to see ELEANOR. Disgusted either by
his friend's cryptic words or with failing to find
ELEANOR, he whips his horse to follow after his
companion at a lope.

EXT   PAYNE PORCH   EARLY EVENING
A loveseat swing sits at the Payne end of the porch. Stationary chairs are at the Straw end. ELEANOR and MARIA rock side by side in wooden rockers in the middle. They are dressed nicely, in anticipation of their husbands' return from the field. For a brief period, they say nothing. MARIA, seemingly resolved to speak her mind, hesitantly speaks.

                    MARIA
          I don't see what you see in him.

                    ELEANOR
          Who?

                    MARIA
          The professor. He's so old, and he's not
          nearly as attractive as John.

                    ELEANOR
               (not willing to discuss it)
          You find John attractive?

                    MARIA
               (defensive)
          Don't change the subject. I just
          think...you owe John some...respect.

                    ELEANOR
          I respect John.

                    MARIA
               (turns defiantly to ELEANOR)
          You come back from an afternoon
          outing with the...the lecherous
          professor, all hot and sweaty, and this

being one of the mildest springs I've known here, and you have the audacity to tell me nothing happened?

ELEANOR
I didn't say that.

MARIA
So, you admit it! Something did happen.

ELEANOR
Yes.

MARIA
Oh my god! And you say you respect John, the man who risks his life daily to support you?

ELEANOR
What happened is not what you think happened, Maria. You're so melodramatic.

MARIA
Perhaps you'd like to enlighten me, then?

Three riders appear just down the street. The men are singing "The Girl I Left Behind." MARIA jumps up and runs to the steps. ELEANOR stands, stepping calmly up to the porch railing.

MARIA (CONT)
They're coming.

ELEANOR
I see that.

The three riders, JOHN, BEN, and CAPTAIN
ORA NASH (30ish, no distinctive ethnicity),
ride right up to the porch, still singing, and
dismount. Nash holds the horses' reins, while
the husbands embrace their wives.

BEN
Did you miss me?

MARIA
Every second.

JOHN
Did you miss me?

ELEANOR
(teasing)
Not one bit.

MARIA looks uncomfortably over at
ELEANOR. Then down to NASH.

MARIA
Who's your new friend?

BEN
Ladies, this new lad is Captain Ora
Nash. And don't let his good looks fool
you. He's one of the toughest men in a
scrape I've ever known. Excepting me
and John, here, of course. Tie those
horses up, Nash, and step on up. I'm
sure, knowing my Maria, that the
women have planned a welcome home
feast for us.

With a general air of merriment, the five disappear into the Straw side of the house.

MONTAGE:
INT STRAW DINING ROOM
The five people circle the dining table. JOHN has his arm around ELEANOR. MARIA sits as close as possible to BEN, who is eating ravenously. ORA sits at the head of the table, singing .ORA finishes the song, and everyone breaks into applause and laughter. Food is spread banquet-like over the table.

INT PAYNE BEDROOM EARLY MORNING
ELEANOR is shaving her face at the wash basin. JOHN pretends to sneak up behind her, wrestling the shaving blade from her hand, then kissing her passionately, getting the cream on ELEANOR's face all over his own. They laugh when they look at each other.

INT OFFICERS' BALLROOM EVENING
The women are all elegantly dressed. The men are in dress uniform. ELEANOR and JOHN waltz, clearly enjoying each other's company. BEN and MARIA dance, too, but not as energetically. NASH, near the refreshment table, sips his punch and watches, focusing his attention on ELEANOR and JOHN. They see him as they pass, and he raises his cup to them.

EXT PAYNE PORCH NIGHT
The five are sitting on the porch. NASH is strumming a guitar and singing. The others, coupled off, listen dreamily. NASH continually looks toward ELEANOR and JOHN. Fireflies dance just off the porch, and NASH's singing is

overshadowed by the night sounds of insects and frogs.

EXT   THE FLINT HILLS DAY
JOHN, ELEANOR (astride, not sidesaddle), and NASH are out for a ride. They ride up the gentle rise of a hill and follow its crest to one end, which overlooks the rolling plains and a small river. As they sit and admire it, NASH admires ELEANOR. JOHN notices with apparent amusement and a touch of sadness.

INT   CUSTERS' PARLOR AFTERNOON
Several of the officers' wives sit about chatting. Nash is seated next to ELEANOR. They are talking amiably with MARIA. LIBBY stands looking out the window. Through the double front windows, we see several officers smoking, one of whom, from the back, could be CUSTER (longish blond hair, blue military shirt and leather leggings). JOHN and BEN's faces can be seen. They are somber, listening intently to CUSTER.

INT   PAYNE BEDROOM   NIGHT
A lamp on the bedside table burns low. JOHN and ELEANOR are cuddled closely under the bed covers, talking in soft voices.

>   ELEANOR
> Is there any real danger?

>   JOHN
> Not here, no.

>   ELEANOR
> I mean for you.

                    JOHN
Every campaign has its inherent
dangers.

                  ELEANOR
Everyone seems to be taking this
campaign to round up the Sioux more
seriously than they have others.

                    JOHN
It just means more time in the field.

                  ELEANOR
But aren't the Sioux talking war?

                    JOHN
That's what we've been fighting already.
They're just holding out a little longer
before they'll give in and move onto the
reservation. Believe me. Sitting Bull is a
wise leader. He'll see this is the best way
for his people.

                  ELEANOR
Would you, if you were in his place?

JOHN doesn't reply. Instead, he looks away for
a moment, then turns back and begins stroking
ELEANOR's hair and face, eventually kissing
her with more and more passion. ELEANOR
responds in kind.

EXT EDGE OF FORT GROUNDS EARLY
MORNING
It's early June. The sun is just rising. Mist covers
the low-lying areas. and long green grass carpets
the earth. Three companies of cavalry soldiers
are lined up, officers in the fore of each

company, heading out of the fort. Wagonloads of supplies follow. In front, a good distance away, CUSTER and LIBBY, accompanied by three or four dogs, ride their horses. CUSTER and his horse seem unusually animated with CUSTER waving his arms and his horse prancing excitedly. The dogs yip and playfully bite at each other as they run about. Several INDIAN SCOUTS (a mixture of Arikara, Crow, and Lakota) follow CUSTER, then the regular troops. Along the road, officers' wives stand and wave with a good amount of dignity. Further along, enlisted men's wives stand, surrounded by children, waving and singing, "The Girl I Left Behind." Even further, toward the outskirts stand large groups of Indians (also composed of mixed Indian nations), solemnly watching the column snake its way toward the horizon.

ELEANOR, standing to one side holding her horse's reins, watches JOHN and his company march by, waving continually at them. Beside her stand NASH, BEN and MARIA. MARIA holds one hand across her stomach as though pregnant and has the other tucked under BEN's arm. The men salute the passing soldiers, especially JOHN.

                    BEN
          Wish I were going. I'd show those
          Indians a thing or two.

                    MARIA
          I'm glad you're not. Junior is glad, too.

               (glancing at ELEANOR)
          I'm sure they'll all return safely though.

ELEANOR
Libby can't stand to be without Autie,
can she?

NASH
Can you stand to be without John?

ELEANOR
I hope I don't have to find out for long.

ELEANOR looks around to avoid seeing JOHN
disappear over the rise, noticing that ELIZA is
the only Custer servant to attend the send off.
ELIZA appears expressionless as she exchanges
glances with ELEANOR.

The enlisted men's wives and children stand
along a scraggily fence that surrounds the
married soldiers' barracks. The women, unlike
the officers' wives, openly cry, some hold infants
and toddlers up to see their fathers one last
time. Several of the children mimic the soldiers
by lining up and marching alongside the troops.
One enterprising child has a piece of cloth tied
to a stick and heads the child troops.

ELEANOR's attention turns back to the
disappearing column of men and horses,
searching for JOHN among them. Finally
spotting him, she waves one last time, then
turns away, leading her horse back toward the
stables. NASH follows suit.

NASH
Why didn't you ride out with John, the
way Libby did with Custer?

ELEANOR
I couldn't. I'm afraid I don't get wrapped
up in all the pageantry and the hero
worship, the way Libby does. Besides, I
hate prolonged goodbyes. They hurt less
if they're quick, like slicing the skin.

NASH
Are you very much in love with John?

ELEANOR
What a strange question to ask a wife. If
she answers yes, the man who asks is
disappointed. If she answers no, the
man who asks thinks less of the woman,
even if he sees an opportunity for
himself.

NASH
I didn't mean to offend you.

ELEANOR
Didn't you?

INT   CUSTER PARLOR   AFTERNOON
LIBBY is pointing to a map spread out on the
center table. Several officers' wives listen
attentively. Even ELEANOR leans close, despite
the proximity of Prof. NEISMAN next to LIBBY.

LIBBY
According to Autie's last letter, they are
here now, at the mouth of the Tongue
River. He said he's not only had success
in fishing from the river, but he shot an
antelope on the march.

NEISMAN
Sounds as if they're having a wonderful
time.

LIBBY
One thing that sobered Autie was a skull
they found in an abandoned village.
They found it next to the remnants of a
cavalry uniform.

FIRST MAJOR WIFE
The savages.

ELEANOR
(stiffening)
Yes, we're so much more civilized. We
not only alleviated the suffering of the
warriors at Washita, we also ended it for
the women and children. Then we end
their horses' misery, as well. We're the
epitome of the milk of human kindness
all right.

NEISMAN
Don't you even care about your
husband's life, Eleanor?

ELEANOR
(standing)
Of course. I've just never had a stomach
for war.

EXT PORCH OF PAYNE HOUSE   EARLY
EVENING
A lamp, fastened to the outer wall, is lit.
ELEANOR and MARIA are rocking. MARIA
knits baby clothes. ELEANOR fans herself. Ben

comes out to stand by the railing and lights a
pipe.

                    BEN
Lovely evening, isn't it?

                    MARIA
Yes, it is.

MARIA stops rocking and puts a hand to her
stomach. She smiles.

                    MARIA (CONT)
Ben Junior is impatient to come out and
play. He just kicked me again.

                    ELEANOR
It must feel so good to feel life growing
inside you. I wish I could have a child.

                    MARIA
                  (laughs)
It took Ben and I nearly eight years,
Eleanor. Be patient, amiga. I'm sure
you'll get your wish.

ELEANOR smiles sadly. Looking down the
street toward the sound of an approaching
horse.
                    BEN
It looks like Nash coming. You girls need
to get together and fix him up with
someone. He's a mighty lonely man.

MARIA giggles. NASH rides his horse up to the
porch and dismounts.

BEN
Evening, Nash. What brings you out
tonight?

NASH
(looking at ELEANOR)
I thought Mrs. Payne could use some
company.

MARIA
(suspicious and scornful)
She's got Ben and I, doesn't she?

NASH
Do you mind my company, Mrs. Straw?

MARIA
(softening)
Not if you sing us a song.

NASH
I didn't bring my guitar.

ELEANOR
Try it *a capella* then.

NASH
Anything you'd like to hear?

ELEANOR
Anything but "The Girl I Left Behind" or
"Nearer, My God, to Thee."

NASH settles on the loveseat-swing and begins
to sing. Night sounds overtake his singing as we
pull further and further away from the porch.

EXT PAYNE PORCH MORNING
It's Independence Day. The parade ground across from the house is decorated, and a portion of the military band plays patriotic songs. Women and children, and people from Manhattan and Junction City, sit in the stands watching the parade of soldiers--the few who are left at the fort. Children set off fireworks. ELEANOR and NASH sit next to each other in the rocking chairs on the porch.

                    ELEANOR
          They should have encountered the Sioux
          by now, shouldn't they?

                    NASH
          More than likely. We'll get news when
          the next steamer comes back down,
          probably in two days. Are you anxious?

                    ELEANOR
          Libby said yesterday that she feels she's
          lost Autie already. She went on to say
          she didn't hold much stock in
          premonitions, though. Do you?

                    NASH
          If a soldier worried about that, he'd
          never go into battle.

                    ELEANOR
          (attempting laughter)
          If a woman acted on premonition, she'd
          never get married.

She looks at NASH, who smiles reassuringly back. He takes her hand and squeezes it. She squeezes back.

ELEANOR (CONT)
I'll never forget how supportive you've
been through this.

NASH
I understand what you're going through.

ELEANOR
You know, I wish you really did.

NASH
(leaning forward)
Believe me when I say I do.

A burst of firecrackers startles them, and two
boys run away laughing.

INT PAYNE BEDROOM EARLY MORNING
ELEANOR is sleeping fitfully. A volley of shots
startles her awake, and she quickly gets out of
bed, running to the window.

EXT PAYNE HOUSE
BEN is leaning out the Straw bedroom window
as ELEANOR peers out.

ELEANOR
What's going on?

BEN
I don't know, but I'll find out.

BEN's head disappears inside. ELEANOR looks
up and down the street, seeing men on
horseback at one end, with women running
about in their nightgowns.

BEN, still pulling up his suspenders, dashes out the front door and down the porch steps. MARIA sticks her head out the bedroom window.

                    MARIA
          Have you seen anything? Are we under
          attack?

                    ELEANOR
          I've only seen soldiers and women. No
          Indians. So I don't think we're under
          attack.

A woman screams in grief. Indian women's voices are raised in a sorrowful trill.

                    MARIA
          Oh my god.

                    ELEANOR
          They've heard. News has come back
          from the West. Bad news.

ELEANOR withdraws.

INT PAYNE BEDROOM
ELEANOR starts to dress, then realizes her face is stubbly.

                    ELEANOR
                  (to herself)
          Damn. This is no time to have to shave.

Quickly, she pours water and lathers up. She hears her front screen door slam shut and the front door open and close. Footsteps, heavy and slow, sound on the stairs.

ELEANOR
Maria, is that you?

MARIA (OS)
(huffing and puffing)
Yes. Can I help you? Are you okay?

ELEANOR
You shouldn't be climbing the stairs in
your condition. Stay downstairs, I'll be
down momentarily.

MARIA (OS)
All right.

ELEANOR is finishing dressing after having
shaved when she hears MARIA talking to
someone at the door.

SOLDIER (OS)
Hello, Mrs. Straw, is Mrs. Payne here?

MARIA (OS)
Yes, she is. She's upstairs dressing. Shall
I get her?

Other footsteps resound on the wooden steps.

MARIA (OS)
Ben? Ben, what's happened?

BEN (OS)
Where's Eleanor?

MARIA (OS)
Upstairs.

The sound of footsteps climbing the stairs makes ELEANOR sit down in defeat on the edge of the bed. BEN peers around the door jamb into the bedroom.

                    BEN
     Eleanor?

                  ELEANOR
     Yes, Ben.

                    BEN
     Eleanor, John's been...

                  ELEANOR
     Killed.

                    BEN
     Yes. I'm so sorry. He went down
     fighting. He fought valiantly to the end.
     He and 200 other men.

                  ELEANOR
     Two hundred?

                    BEN
     It was a massacre.

ELEANOR begins to cry softly. BEN doesn't know what to do.

                 BEN (CONT)
     Maria, come up here. I think Eleanor
     needs you.

INT   STAIRS
NASH helps MARIA carefully up the stairs.

INT   BEDROOM
Both enter the bedroom and sit on either side of
ELEANOR. NASH looks up at BEN, who has
remained by the door.

                    NASH
        Go on. We'll take care of her.

ELEANOR leans on NASH and cries on his
shoulder. He embraces her, rocking her gently.
MARIA stands and crosses to BEN. She has
almost reached him, when she grabs her
stomach in pain.

                    BEN
        Maria. Are you all right?

ELEANOR stops crying. She and NASH rush to
help BEN ease MARIA to the floor.

                    MARIA
        I think it's time.

                    BEN
        Are you sure? It's too early.

MARIA cries out in pain again. Her water
breaks and spills all over the floor. They all
look at each other incredulously.

                    ELEANOR
        Let's put her on the bed. Ora, go get a
        doctor. Ben, have whoever is still
        downstairs put some water on to boil,
        and you get some sheets out of that
        trunk over there.

The two men carry MARIA to the bed, then disappear out the door. ELEANOR begins soothing MARIA who is panicking.

                    MARIA
It's too early. By my calculations, I should have another month and a half yet.

                    ELEANOR
These things are never exact. Don't worry. My mother always told me I took twelve months to be born and twenty-five years to grow up. You're going to have a healthy, happy baby, amiga.

MARIA laughs, then cries out in pain.

INT   PAYNE BEDROOM   NIGHT
MARIA cries out in pain, panting heavily as she lies in the bed. She is covered in sweat. ELEANOR and LIBBY assist the doctor—ELEANOR wipes MARIA's brow; LIBBY, looking strained but pulled together after the loss of her husband, stands ready with fresh sheets--discarded bloody ones are piled on the floor.

                    DOCTOR
You're doing just fine, Maria. I can see his head crowning now. You can push.

                    LIBBY
Push, dear. Push as hard as you can.

                    MARIA
                (with much effort)
I'm pushing. I'm pushing.

ELEANOR tries to watch what is happening between MARIA's legs but can't stomach it for long. She concentrates on smiling at MARIA.

> ELEANOR
> You have names all picked out, don't you?

> MARIA
> Benjamin Junior, if it's a boy.

> (MARIA pushes hard)
> Eleanor Meredith, if it's a girl.

> LIBBY
> Eleanor? Why not Elizabeth? Or Libby?

LIBBY laughs weakly at her own joke, and everyone else joins in, both because they feel they must and because they are relieved that LIBBY is soldiering on. MARIA cries out and bears down. The baby finally slides out. The doctor passes it off to LIBBY.

> DOCTOR
> Eleanor it is, Maria.

> MARIA
> It's a girl? Is she all right?

> LIBBY
> (as she wipes off the tiny baby)
> Ten fingers, ten toes.

MARIA cries out again and bears down again, just as the baby cries.

                    ELEANOR
          What's happening, doctor?

                    DOCTOR
          She should be passing the placenta now.

                    (looks)
          Oh my god.

                    MARIA
          Oh my god, what?!

                    DOCTOR
          There's another one coming.

ELEANOR smiles excitedly at MARIA. LIBBY
hands the swaddled baby girl to ELEANOR, who
takes her somewhat awkwardly, then begins to
cuddle and talk to the baby, showing her to
MARIA. LIBBY readies new sheets for the
second baby, smiling, fighting tears, as she takes
it from the doctor.

                    LIBBY
          This one's Ben Junior.

As she swaddles the baby, LIBBY tries to dry
her own tears.

EXT PAYNE PORCH AFTERNOON, THREE
MONTHS LATER
BEN and MARIA, each holding a baby—the girl
in pink, the boy in blue—swing in the loveseat.
NASH stands on a porch step near ELEANOR,
who, although she's dressed in mourning, is
leaning against the railing admiring the babies.

ELEANOR
I still wish I could have a baby.

BEN
You're young yet. I'm sure you'll
remarry. Right, Nash?

NASH
Yes, I'm sure when the right man comes
along, Eleanor, you'll be ready to marry
again.

ELEANOR
I'll never find another man like John.

NASH
I know I'm a poor substitute for John,
but would you consider going to the
dance next Saturday with me?

MARIA
Yes, Eleanor. You haven't gotten out at
all in the last three months. You need to
start living again.

ELEANOR
It was nice of the Army to agree to put
me up for six months, wasn't it?

NASH
They'd keep you longer, if you wanted to
stay.

   (moves up to sit next to her)
Will you just agree to go to the dance
with me? Please?

MARIA AND BEN
(together)
Go. Have fun.

Everyone laughs. ELEANOR throws up her hands in defeat and nods her head. The babies begin to cry.

INT OFFICERS BALLROOM EVENING
The military band plays as officers and their wives or dates dance. The room is decorated with regimental regalia. A refreshment table sits at one end. It is covered with various finger foods and a glass punch bowl with several glass cups.

NASH is in his dress uniform as he escorts ELEANOR, who is wearing a yellow dress, into the room. He motions toward the dancers, and, after a few greetings, they join the dancers. Dancers whirl past the refreshment table—with each sweep more food disappears. When there is little food left, we return our focus on ELEANOR and NASH, who finish dancing and applaud the band along with the few other couples remaining. ELEANOR fans herself and motions toward the door. They step out on the veranda.

EXT VERANDA NIGHT
A couple of officers, who are smoking, are grouped together near the door. One couple stands next to the rail a little way down. ELEANOR leads NASH further down where they lean on the railing, looking out over the parade grounds.

                    NASH
I'm glad you came.

                  ELEANOR
So am I.

                    NASH
I think you're wonderful.

                  ELEANOR
You find me full of wonder?

                    NASH
I wonder how long it'll be before you let
me kiss you.

                  ELEANOR
You don't want to kiss me.

                    NASH
Why don't I?

                  ELEANOR
It's a long story, and I'm afraid you
wouldn't understand. Let's walk, shall
we?

ELEANOR leads NASH down the stairs and
onto the parade grounds.

EXT   PARADE GROUNDS   NIGHT
ELEANOR heads for the row of cannons, which
sit at one end of the field. She stops and leans
against the wheel of the third one, looking at the
stars.
                  ELEANOR
Tell me, Capt. Nash, what do you see for
the future?

NASH
Our future? Or that of our country?
ELEANOR
Our world.

NASH
That's a pretty big place.

ELEANOR
Makes you feel small, doesn't it?

NASH
Not when I'm next to you.

ELEANOR
(laughing)
You have a romantic response for
everything, don't you?

NASH
Especially to you.

ELEANOR
I'm really flattered, Ora, I really am,
but...I'm not the kind of woman you
think I am.

NASH
What kind of woman is that?

ELEANOR
You don't want to know.

NASH
I wish you'd quit telling me I don't want
to know something, dammit. I have a
mind of my own. Eyes and ears, too, for
that matter.

(pauses)
And I know who you are.
ELEANOR
(paying attention)
You do? Who am I, then?

NASH
You're the future Mrs. Nash.

ELEANOR
(exasperated)
Really? Who made you lord and master
over my fate?

NASH
John.

ELEANOR looks puzzled and angry. She starts
to speak when NASH interrupts her.

NASH
He and I were more than friends. Much
more.

ELEANOR
What do you mean? Much more?

NASH
(uncomfortable)
In the field, we were to each other what
you two were to each other here.

                    ELEANOR
                 (fierce whisper)
          He slept with you?

                    NASH
          In every sense of the word.

                    ELEANOR
          How? Why?
                    NASH
          Military men often share blankets—for
          warmth, usually. Sometimes it becomes
          more. We...we had more.

                    ELEANOR
          How long... ? Why didn't he ever tell
          me?

                    NASH
          He wasn't sure how much of a woman
          you had become. He didn't know how
          you'd take it.

                    ELEANOR
          Son of a bitch. The little.... Cheating on
          me.

ELEANOR, in her anger, starts to walk away.
NASH quickly follows.

                    NASH
          He always spoke highly of you. He never
          wanted to hurt you.

NASH reaches out and stops ELEANOR.

                    NASH (CONT)
          I wouldn't have told you now, but...

ELEANOR
But what?

NASH
I wanted you to know what I am
because...

ELEANOR
Because...?

NASH
I've loved you since I first saw you. I'd be
honored if you'd be my...wife.

ELEANOR looks up at the stars.

INT FORT CHAPEL DAY
Dressed in her best white dress, ELEANOR and
NASH exchange vows. MARIA and BEN,
holding their babies, sit in the pews. LIBBY and
the other officers' wives sit on the bride's side.
Officers sit on the groom's. Pushing back her
small veil, NASH softly kisses ELEANOR, and
they walk down the aisle as friends congratulate
them along the way. NEISMAN sits in the
corner of the chapel.

INT NASH BEDROOM NIGHT
ELEANOR, still in her wedding dress, sits at a
small desk in front of the window, writing in her
diary. NASH comes in and stands behind her,
putting his hands on her shoulders, then rubs
her neck. She stops writing and stands, facing
him. They undress each other slowly, then climb
into bed together. NASH reaches up and turns
down the lamp.

RETURN TO OPENING FRAME

INT UNDERTAKER'S WORKROOM
MORNING
The undertaker sits, eating his lunch. ELEANOR's corpse lies covered by a sheet on a long table in the center of the room. The undertaker wipes his mouth and stands when two older men, the HEAD PHYSICIAN for the military hospital and the fort's CHAPLAIN, enter the room.

                    CHAPLAIN
          Is there something wrong with Mrs.
          Nash's body, sergeant?

                    UNDERTAKER
          Yes, sir, there is.

                    DOCTOR
          What is it, man, we haven't got all day.
          I've other flu victims to attend to who
          are still alive.

                    UNDERTAKER
          All I need to know, sirs, is what to do
          about this.

The UNDERTAKER sweeps back the sheet. Both men register shock with the CHAPLAIN looking to the doctor for reassurance of what he sees.

                    DOCTOR
          I assume Captain Nash knows about
          this.

CHAPLAIN
It's most likely he does.

DOCTOR
Does anyone else know?

UNDERTAKER
As far as I know, just me.

CHAPLAIN
It's a pity. Capt. Nash is due for
promotion soon, too.

DOCTOR
(addressing chaplain)
You know how news of this would make
the Army look, don't you?

CHAPLAIN
Of course, but...

DOCTOR
No buts. Word of this isn't to go beyond
this room. Do I make myself clear,
reverend?

CHAPLAIN
Yes, sir.

DOCTOR
Sergeant?

UNDERTAKER
Yes, sir. Will you sign the certificate of
death?

DOCTOR
Of course.

(DOCTOR signs then continues.)
Word has been sent to Nash?

                    UNDERTAKER
Not yet, sir. He's in Oklahoma Territory.
A wire will be sent directly.

                      DOCTOR
Fine. Then stop over at the Nash
quarters and see if she kept a diary or
journal, just in case. If you find one,
burn it. Reverend, see to the funeral
arrangements, will you?

        (DOCTOR as he's leaving)
Make it a nice ceremony. He was a good
woman.

AS END CREDITS ROLL

INT NASH BEDROOM AFTERNOON
The UNDERTAKER searches the bedroom,
rifling through drawers, searching under the
bed, groping pillows, but finds nothing. The
camera sees: a Chinese painting of a man with
an erection groping a woman. Behind the
picture is a wooden door. Behind the door is a
cubby hole. In the cubby hole is ELEANOR's
JOURNAL, which sits partially over the two
certificates of marriage.

TO BLACK

About the Author

Ruth J. Heflin grew up in a small town in Kansas, the 10th of 10 children, the 7th of 7 daughters.

Her father was the family storyteller, but her mother took her twice a month to the local library where she enjoyed checking out exactly eight books at a time. Ruth loved reading, having the great fortune of having many teachers help her learn the skill, so that she was proficient in reading, writing, and counting to 100 well before she began kindergarten.

As a robust young girl, Ruth loved reading, writing, drawing, riding horses, running around the family farm, and playing with her dog. Every morning, she helped feed the livestock, which included rabbits, chickens, ducks, cattle, her horse, and pigs, before going to school, a chore she did twice a day all the way through high school. After she bought her own horse while in high school, she rode her horse, Misty, every evening after her chores were done.

Because of her size and assertive demeanor, running down a few basemen during sports when they refused to move, Ruth was nicknamed Moose by older boys in high school, but also Encyclo by her friends because one of her favorite habits was to sit in front of the tall bookcase her father had built that housed three different sets of encyclopedias and read them. When she did not understand a concept, she used another encyclopedia to look it up, resulting in her having a phenomenal knowledge of many things even as a teenager.

Ruth's love of learning pushed her through three college degrees, a bachelor's degree, a master's degree, and a doctorate—wherein she studied America's various ethnic cultures and gender. She also worked at Fort Riley one summer while pursuing her master's degree at Kansas State University, which is why she chose to set Mrs. Nash's story in those places.

Ruth first learned about Mrs. Nash, who actually lived at Fort Lincoln, Nebraska, while working on her doctorate at Oklahoma State University, but she studied various forms of transgendering, which has been labeled variously during her studies. Realizing that Mrs. Nash was the earliest verifiable reference to an EuroAmerican male who chose to present as female in American history (aka the first colorless trans woman), Ruth designed this screenplay, originally, as an ironic homage to Alfred Hitchcock's "wrong man" theme that runs through most of his films.

www.choeofpleirnpress.com
choeofpleirnpress@gmail.com